LOVE KINDLED

A REGENCY NOVELETTE

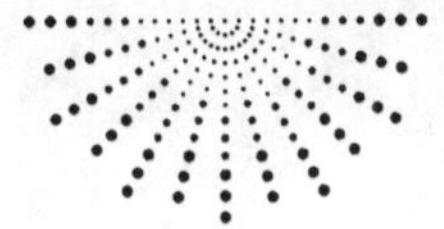

ROSIE CHAPEL

Love Kindled
A Regency Novelette

First printing: 2021
ISBN: 978-0-6451116-8-2 (e-book)
ISBN: 978-0-6451116-9-9 (paperback)

Ulfire Pty. Ltd.
P.O. Box 1481
South Perth
WA 6951
Australia

www.rosiechapel.com

Cover Designed by Lisa Miller with Got You Covered
Image of couple courtesy Period Images

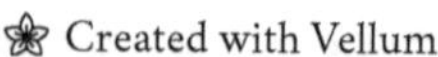 Created with Vellum

Although penned for the anthology in which Love Kindled was originally included, I think the sentiment holds.

This book is dedicated to everyone who has faced hardship of any kind, and found the strength within to rebuild.

ACKNOWLEDGMENTS

Grateful thanks to Lilly Rayman, for inviting me to contribute to the Building Love Anthology, in which this story was originally published.
My gratitude to Angie Wade at Novel Nurse Editing for her keen eye.
Heartfelt appreciation to Lisa Miller with Got You Covered for this gorgeous cover.

An extra special shout out to my wonderful hubby for his endless support and technical wizardry. I have known him more than four decades, and this month we celebrate our pearl anniversary — an occasion I deem worthy of mention. A part of him is in every one of my heroes, and the love he kindled all those years ago still burns bright.

CHAPTER ONE

LONDON ~ MAY 1816

It was all Lady Amelia Gresham could do not to scream. Here was she, newly widowed, Hayward barely cold in his grave, and already they were talking about marrying her off to that boor, Ambrose.

For the last hour or so, she had sat quietly while everyone talked around her. Her head was beginning to ache and her temper to seethe. Apparently, even as a widow she had no voice, or so they thought.

Amelia stood, drew herself up to her considerable height, and coughed.

It took several moments before anyone acknowledged her presence, which only served to vex her further.

"Might I be permitted to speak?" she asked, her tone dangerously bland.

The Marquis of Hungerford, Amelia's father-in-law, turned his flinty gaze on her, continuing to argue that marriage to Ambrose was the perfect solution.

Nobody had ever seen fit to ask her opinion, not once in her whole life, and Amelia was tired of being ignored. She wasn't stupid. Daughters of nobility were pawns in their father's schemes to bolster influence or wealth. The better the match, the higher the status.

Frivolous emotions such as love or tenderness, or even respect were not considered essential to any discussion. Aware some unions drifted along quite nicely, as far as Amelia could tell, the majority lacked any affection whatsoever.

Her own marriage had been soulless. It was not that had they disliked each other. Dislike suggested some strength of feeling or concern in the other's well-being was involved, even if it were negative. Amelia and Hayward had been utterly indifferent to one another. So indifferent, they could not summon up enough interest to consummate their nuptials. A detail Amelia was determined to keep to herself.

Hayward Ingram, Earl of Gresham, had died a week previously, following a duel with one of his rivals in the racing fraternity. Amelia hated horse racing with a passion and, even though a competent horsewoman, wasn't overly enamoured of the creatures at all, except as a means to an end.

She struggled to understand what had prompted the rash challenge, especially given the outcome. The two involved were grievously injured, Hayward fatally so, although Amelia had heard it was likely her husband's opponent would survive.

Now here she was, a widow at three and twenty. Looking back over her life, Amelia realised she had never done anything impetuous or spontaneous. Her behaviour — always that expected by her somewhat overbearing parents — one of sedate refinement. It did not behove her to ruffle the surface.

Of late, an almost uncontrollable urge to defy all conventions and constraints had begun to stir within her. The tug of freedom — tantalising. Hayward's unfortunate demise had opened a door just wide enough for her to see beyond the confines of her limited world, and she would prefer it did not slam shut. Not just yet.

Straightening her shoulders, Amelia stepped forward.

In deference to her father-in-law, she executed a deep curtsy. "My lord, am I not entitled to a period of mourning? Gresham is hardly buried, and you are arranging his replacement. I do believe you owe him and me a little respect." Her tones a trifle more assertive than usual.

There were hushed gasps from the other three in the room. Amelia's mother-in-law, Lady Priscilla Hungerford. Ambrose, currently Viscount Hastings but in line to inherit his father's earldom. Mr Williams, the Hungerfords' solicitor, who was present to read Hayward's will.

Their brief and uneventful marriage notwithstanding, it transpired her husband had ensured — all things remaining equal — Amelia should be comfortable in the unfortunate event of him dying prior to inheriting the marquisate.

Lamentably, Hayward had not taken into consideration his own vices.

"It is imperative we keep the Hungerford assets within the family." Lord Hungerford was reluctant to continue. Money was a delicate subject, and women were usually excluded from any discussion regarding finances.

Amelia knew to what he alluded.

"My lord, I am cognisant of my husband's debts."

Lord Hungerford narrowed his eyes, wary now.

Amelia noticed Mr Williams bite his lip to prevent a smile. She had spent many hours with the solicitor, prior to and since her husband's death, and knew everything about the financial straits of the family.

Hayward had been an inveterate gambler and a bad one. Money slipped through his fingers like water, leaving Amelia to control what she could in order to prevent the Gresham estates falling into rack and ruin. The solicitor was a font of knowledge, undaunted by Amelia's questions, his help invaluable.

Until her marriage, Amelia was shielded from the business aspects being a member of the *ton* entailed. Ladies should not bother their, obviously, empty heads with important matters. Amelia discovered, to her surprise, she possessed an uncanny knack for understanding how to manage an estate and — unbeknownst to the rest of her husband's family — with Mr Williams' assistance, had kept Gresham Park afloat.

There was absolutely no chance of her giving that up. Not without a fight.

An idea had begun percolating during the morning, and for once, Amelia was determined to get her own way.

"I have long been aware of Gresham's gambling. How could I not know? He was frittering away his money as though it grows on trees. I was the one left to safeguard the estate and work out how to pay staff with the pitiful sum he left available to me each month," she paused. "I have a proposition to make."

Lord Hungerford regarded her steadily, his aristocratic visage showing no expression. After a long moment, he inclined his head. "Speak, woman, but make it quick."

"I have been a dutiful daughter and, for the last two years, wife. I maintained Gresham Park, despite your son's best intents, and expect it to turn a slight profit during the coming year. I am frugal and recently employed an eminently reliable steward, in whose hands I can trust the management of the estate.

"While I am pleased with my efforts, they came at no little cost to me. In light of recent events, I am resolved to give myself time to adjust. I have a hankering to travel. To see something of this England in which we live but are rarely afforded the chance to appreciate.

"I shall take six months. Upon my return, I may — I only say may — be prepared to engage in discussion regarding a possible marriage to Ambrose. However…"

Amelia raised her hand as her father-in-law interrupted, stuttering and stammering at her audacity.

"I am a widow and a countess in my own right. I am wearied of being dictated to, of allowing others to decide my fate. While I had no control, my hands were tied. That ends today. I have reached my majority. My life is my life, and you have no cause to instruct me. Hayward's will made that clear."

Amelia was trembling with anxiety at her recklessness but held her nerve. She refused to remain silent anymore. To speak thus was liberating, prompting another decision. Not only was she going to implement her plan, but also it would be without the trappings of luxury. She fixed her gaze on Lord Hungerford.

They studied each other for several seconds, and it was Hayward's father who dropped his gaze first.

A small victory but no less rewarding.

Mr Williams cleared his throat, the sound breaking through an atmosphere already strained.

"May I suggest we conclude our business? 'Tis not a comfortable subject, and I have no desire to prolong it."

Hungerford nodded, and the affable solicitor explained the last few particulars of the will. He was about to take his leave when Amelia requested a moment of his time.

Without waiting for permission, she tucked her arm through his, and led him through the open French doors, onto the terrace.

"Mr Williams, I would like to thank you for all your help and ask that you keep me apprised of any… err… untoward developments. If I find somewhere to stay for more than a week, I will inform you of my address. Mr Halifax, my steward, has your details should he require any advice, but he has proven to be efficient and trustworthy. I do not foresee any problems."

Mr Williams patted her hand. "I hope you have a pleasant sojourn, Lady Gresham. I wish Lord Hungerford knew of your tireless efforts to protect his good name. Alas, the nobility often cannot see past the end of their own noses." He dropped a sly wink, making Amelia chuckle.

She shrugged her shoulders. "'Tis of no matter. The important thing is now I have said my piece, I can leave as soon as is practicable. For the next six months, I will no longer be Lady Gresham. I shall use my maiden name and become, temporarily at least, Mrs Amelia Danneville."

She grinned, a wholly unaffected gesture.

To the elderly solicitor, it was as though she was bathed in the glow of a hundred candles.

"I trust you find what it is you seek," he said quietly.

Pressing her hand one more time he bowed, walked back into the study, collected his papers, and said his goodbyes.

Amelia leant against the frame of the elegant door, admiring the pretty garden, ruminating over his words. *Was she seeking something?* It was conceivable, but what she had yet to discern.

Shaking her head, she turned her back on the profusion of blossoms and faced her father-in-law.

&.

Two days and at least three acrimonious exchanges later, Amelia departed Hungerford House en route to Gresham Park. Hayward's father had tried every trick in the book to dissuade her from, what he referred to as, her lunatic scheme.

Finally, he had accepted she was steadfast. To be fair he, albeit grudgingly, wished her well, pleading with her to consider marriage to Ambrose while away.

In spite of Lord Hungerford's cantankerous disposition, he had a soft spot for Amelia and, in truth, only wanted what he believed to be the best for her.

He came from a world where women were little more than chattels to be married off to the wealthiest or most influential bidder. To have his decisions thwarted was a shock. His own wife, while perfectly lovely, would not dream of questioning anything her husband did or said.

He would never admit it, but Lord Hungerford held a secret admiration for Amelia's fortitude and, following her departure was stunned to discover precisely how capable she had been in overseeing his son's property.

Amelia heaved a sigh of relief when her carriage rattled out of London and turned up the Great North Road. Her journey would take two or three days, depending on the weather and state of the roads. This time of the year, with spring rains, they could be treacherous.

Her faithful maid, Jenny, accompanied her, as did Trotter, her driver and stalwart defender. The hood was down, the day bright, and Amelia, breathing in the clean fresh country air, began to relax for the first time in as long as she could remember.

CHAPTER TWO

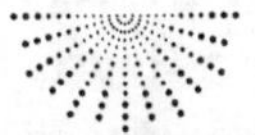

CAMBRIDGESHIRE ~ JUNE 1816

It did not seem like a month since Amelia's return to Gresham Park. Originally intending to embark on her mini grand tour within a week of her arrival, it ended up being rather longer.

Estate matters arose which required her attention and, as frustrating as they were, Amelia was pleased she had been there to deal with the problems.

At last, she was on her way.

Consternation would be rife among her London friends if they saw Amelia now. By dint of scraping her gloriously rich and naturally wavy, dark-blonde hair into a tight bun, and wearing drab-coloured clothes, the elegant and beautiful Lady Amelia Gresham had transformed herself into plain Mrs Danneville, widow.

Her bombazine gown was somewhere between grey and black. She couldn't quite bring herself to wear the severe black of mourning; the grey was bad enough. For one thing, it didn't suit her, and for another, she felt it disrespectful.

She did not mourn Hayward. She was sorry he had died, saddened for his parents, but she wasn't lamenting a lost love, she wasn't even grieving for a friend. If she was honest, she felt relieved. Now, she didn't have to waste the rest of her life in a loveless marriage.

Moreover, she had absolutely no intention of marrying Ambrose, especially given his recent behaviour. The evening before she left Hungerford House, he had cornered her. His advances were less than courtly, and he claimed his conduct acceptable because they were virtually betrothed.

Amelia had kicked him in the shin and thwacked him across the nose. Spitting with fury, she had declared if he ever tried such a thing again, he would rue the day he was born. Ambrose had laughed in her face and walked… or rather, hobbled… away.

The encounter left her feeling vulnerable yet determined *never* to be subject to his questionable predilections.

Better late than not at all, here she was on a warm June morning, setting out on her adventure. A deep, blood-red wrap, grey bonnet, and grey boots completed her sensible travelling ensemble. Amelia realised, if she stepped into the shadows, she might disappear altogether. An image that made her giggle almost uncontrollably.

She had no particular destination in mind, thinking she might travel towards the Cotswolds, hopefully staying a little while in Cirencester and Bath. She also wanted to see Stone-henge and maybe the New Forest. It was wonderful not to have anything specific planned. A bubble of excitement threatened to burst out in a wild laugh or unladylike whoop. Ever refined, Amelia satisfied herself with a quick clap of her hands.

Cirencester ~ June 1816

They had been travelling for the better part of four days when the carriage pulled up in front of a large coaching inn bearing the regal name of The Lion and Eagle.

Amelia, now heartily sick of being rattled about, was pondering the possibility of finding a guesthouse in Cirencester. A place to unpack properly. A base from where she could explore the surrounding countryside.

Wearily, she stepped down, thanking Trotter who affirmed he would bring the luggage and settle the horses. Walking into the inn, Amelia was hard pressed not to wrinkle her nose at the smell of unwashed bodies.

Innate politeness came to the fore and, disciplining her features, she approached the innkeeper.

"I am looking for a room for two nights if I may." She smiled at the portly gentleman, who nodded absently. "Along with a hot meal for my driver and myself."

"Not a problem," he replied, running an appraising eye over her, "my lady."

Amelia shook her head. "Thank you, sir and, Mrs Danneville will suffice."

The man wasn't convinced, but he didn't argue. What these odd folk wanted to be called was no concern of his, as long as they paid. He called for a serving maid, with whom he had a muttered conversation. The young girl bobbed a curtsy, and led Amelia up two flights of stairs and along a gallery overlooking the central courtyard to a room at the far end.

"'Tis quieter 'ere, miss," the girl said. "It gets a bit loud in them rooms over't bar. You shouldn't be disturbed by drunks either."

"Thank you…" Amelia raised an eyebrow.

"Ruby, miss," the girl supplied, bobbing a curtsy.

"Thank you, Ruby. Might I ask you to direct my man up here, please? He will be bringing my luggage. His name is Trotter."

Ruby confirmed she would.

Amelia, who had never patronised a coaching inn in her life, was unsure what to do at this point so slipped the girl a coin. From the beam on Ruby's face, it was as though she had given her a fortune. Hopefully, it would ensure a half-decent meal.

Smiling, Amelia said she would be down for something to eat forthwith.

"Just pop your 'ead round, and I'll get you a proper table in the parlour, like." Ruby assured her and tripped back along the walkway.

&a.

The next morning following a reasonable night's sleep, Amelia took the carriage into Cirencester. Primarily, to look around the town, but also to see whether she could locate a guesthouse.

A lover of history, Amelia already knew Cirencester dated back to Roman times, was originally known as Corinium Dobunnorum, and later became a hub for the wool trade.

While exploring the town, she discovered, once upon a time, there was an abbey, which was founded in the twelfth century, and subsequently destroyed by Henry VIII. Further, during the English Civil War, the opposing sides fought up and down these very streets with three hundred killed, and over a thousand held captive in the church.

Today, it was far more peaceful. A thriving market town, easily accessible by the network of turnpike roads at which Cirencester was the centre. Amelia strolled about happily, soaking up the ancient atmosphere.

She was drawn to the beautiful parish church which, cathedral-like in size, was a remarkable sight.

Amelia lingered a while in its serene coolness before taking the time to admire the spectacular fan vaulting in the south porch, interested to note the tower was also used as a town hall. The day passed in the blink of an eye, and before she knew it, it was mid-afternoon.

Tired, Amelia realised she had not found anywhere to lodge. It was too late now, so she postponed that task until the morrow. Upon returning to the inn, she greeted Mr Meadows, the innkeeper, and requested a hot meal be served in the parlour within the hour.

A quick freshen up in her bedchamber, and Amelia made her way to the patrons' private parlour. She was relaxing, a tankard of beer in her hand — something up until the previous day had not tasted, but found she was partial to — when a whirlwind blew in through the glass double doors.

"Catherine, please, sweetheart. Y—" A deep voice, whose tones sounded slightly unhinged, was cut off by a shriek.

"No. *No*. **No**. I will not. I hate them, and I hate you."

A veritable virago of an imp, her short curls bouncing

around her head, stood, with hands on hips, cheeks bright red, and lips pursed. She was glowering at whomever had caused what was, undoubtedly, an indefensible faux pas.

Looking to be scarcely more than three or four years old, the tot wagged her finger at approaching footsteps.

"I will scream, and then you will be sorry."

Amelia stared in fascination at the child, who seemed certain to carry out her threat. In fact, she drew in a deep breath and was on the verge of expelling it in the promised bellow when Amelia burst out laughing.

The golden notes echoed around the room and floated along the corridor, arresting the advance of a formidable gentleman intent on teaching his rebellious daughter a lesson in manners.

As he reached the door, he noticed a woman of homely appearance wearing a dull gown, peels of mirth falling from her lips.

Catherine, said daughter, was so shocked, all thoughts of screaming vanished, and she gaped at the woman who dared laugh at her.

"Are you laughing at me?" she demanded truculently.

"Yes, yes, I suppose I am. Oh, my dear, you are not old enough to be throwing tantrums. What on earth prompted it?" Amelia asked, amusement clear in her voice.

Catherine cocked her head and studied the stranger, seriously.

"My papa."

"Your papa upset you? That seems improbable. What did he do?"

Intrigued, the gentleman waited to hear his daughter's answer.

"He wanted me to have a bath." Her disgust suggested this was the worst punishment *ever* to be inflicted on a poor, unsuspecting child.

"Am I to suppose you do not like baths?"

The nice lady sounded interested. Encouraged, Catherine inched closer and leant against Amelia's knee.

She shook her head. "No," she confided. "They make you wet."

Catherine propped her elbows on Amelia's leg and rested her chin on her palms. Such an adult pose, and it was all Amelia could do not to laugh again.

"I see. Yes, I imagine that could present a problem."

Amelia caught movement out of the corner of her eye and raised her head, spying a tall, harassed, and rumpled-looking gentleman peering around the doorway. He *had* to be the child's father; they both sported the same wayward hair.

Her lips curving ever-so slightly at the corners, Amelia shook her head, indicating that he not intrude, and caught his answering nod as he stepped back out of sight.

Casually, Amelia sipped her beer. "I like baths myself," she said almost as an aside. "I love to soak in the scented water and wash my hair, then when I'm all clean and dry, and wearing a fresh gown, I sit by the fire to dry my hair. All in all, a wonderfully relaxing experience."

. . .

The man standing in the corridor listened carefully, trying to ignore the image the woman's words evoked in his head, despite her staid appearance.

He was at his wit's end. His daughter was a wilful child, thoroughly spoilt, and he struggled to know how to deal with her petulance. She thwarted him at every turn and constantly refused to do anything he asked; honestly, she was worse than an unbroken horse.

He loved her dearly and tried to make up for the fact it was only him. Her mother… well, that was another story entirely… suffice it to say she had never been part of Catherine's life. He wrenched his attention back to the conversation going on in the parlour.

"Why does your papa wish you to have a bath today?" Amelia asked, curiously, for the child looked quite presentable.

"I jumped in the pond, and he thought it was dirty." The child pondered this for a moment. "I like mud though. 'Tis warm between your toes."

Amelia could not contain her merriment. She leant back and let it come, as the child lifted her leg to reveal a shoe and, what presumably had once been, a white stocking, liberally caked with black mud.

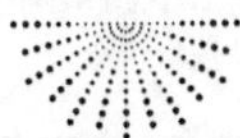

CHAPTER THREE

"Your papa is correct. You cannot possibly go to bed with all that mud on you. Think of the poor maid who will have to wash your sheets," Amelia said, trying to swallow her giggles.

"'Tis their job to clean things," the little girl responded, imperiously, her small chin jutting out.

"That may be the case, but you should not make their life any harder than it already is. How many guests do you think might be staying here?"

The child mulled this over. Spreading out her hands, she ventured, "Lots?"

"Lots and lots, and the staff have to work very quickly to make sure every guest has clean bedding." Amelia didn't believe this for a second, but that so small a child thought nothing of burdening maids with extra work, troubled her. "If you dirty the sheets when you could have washed off the mud, you will make their day much harder."

She reached out to take the girl's hands in hers. "The people who take care of us are very important, for they make our lives easier. We must respect them. Do you understand?" she said gently, but firmly.

Catherine stared at Amelia then nodded slowly, whispering, "Please, would you help me in the bath?"

"What about your nanny? Or your mama, or even papa?" Surely the girl's family had staff with them.

"I do not have a Mama, and Nanny left…" the child trailed off.

Amelia hesitated, chewing on her bottom lip. It wasn't that she didn't want to help the little girl, but she was a stranger and, thus, probably not the most suitable person to be bathing someone else's daughter.

In the corridor, the tall gentleman had been listening. Something about the way this woman spoke with Catherine — and his daughter's responses — prompted an interesting idea to germinate.

"I wonder?" he mused and stepped forward into the parlour.

"Good afternoon." He bowed, taking in the scene.

The woman was sitting by the window, a half-drunk beer on the table. She looked refined but her attire gave nothing away. Loath to address her incorrectly, he erred on the side of caution.

"My lady. I do apologise for my daughter's discourteous interruption."

Amelia smiled lightly, amused by his harried appearance. "'Tis of no matter, sir. We have been enjoying a lovely conversation about baths."

"Papa, Papa, please may she bath me?" The child flicked her hand towards Amelia as she entreated her father.

"Calling a lady 'she' is not polite, Catherine," he chastised mildly. "You know you are supposed to address them by their title…" He raised a quizzical eyebrow.

"Mrs Danneville," Amelia supplied.

"Pleased to make your acquaintance, Mrs Danneville. L…" He hesitated. "Rupert Latimer at your service, and this is my rather headstrong daughter, Catherine or, as we usually call her, Cate. Cate, Mrs Danneville."

Cate curtseyed neatly. For all her truculence, it was clear someone had taught the child her manners.

Amelia stood from her chair and dropped a curtsy of her own, the dark grey of her dress flowing around her, reminding Rupert Latimer of ripples in a pond on a cloudless night.

"Papa, pleeeeeeease may Mrs Dan… Davn… Dandelion bath me?"

Cate's mistake with her name tickled Amelia who, prudently, did not draw attention to it.

"She understands baths." The child widened her eyes and batted her sooty lashes winsomely in a bid to win over her father, who was glad of the distraction.

Amelia watched as Mr — *was it Mr or Lord?* — Latimer's grave expression became one of gentle tenderness. The change, startling. Something inside Amelia mimicked Cate's fluttering lashes, a sensation she did not recognise.

Paying it no mind, she glanced up at Mr Latimer and shrugged her shoulders. "If you trust me, a stranger, with your daughter, I would be glad to help. That said, I do not wish to overstep the bounds of propriety should there be another who would normally bath her."

The man's lips curled in a cynical smile. "There is no mother or maid, and Cate is correct. Her nanny left." Unsure why he had shared personal information, Rupert heaved a weary sigh. His brow creased. "I am unable to keep a nanny more than a month. Cate has driven every single one away."

Amelia's fingers itched to smooth his forehead. "Well," she said, in practical tones, "naught we can do about that now. Time is passing. Let us organise this bath." She rang for a maid, and within two minutes Ruby peeped into the parlour.

"Is there something you need, miss?" She dipped a curtsy.

Amelia explained, and remembered to ask whether her meal might be delayed.

Ruby nodded, confirming she would arrange to have a bath taken up to his lordship's room with all haste.

Amelia thanked her, arching an eyebrow at Cate's father. "His lordship is it? Pray tell, was there a reason you saw fit to introduce yourself without including your title?" Blithely ignoring the fact, she was doing exactly the same thing.

He grinned, sheepishly. "'Tis nice, on the few occasions I can get away with it, to pretend I am just a man taking his daughter on a holiday. Not to have people behave in the obsequious manner they cannot seem to help, the moment they discover you are nobility. In truth, I am Lord Badlesmere."

Familiar with his title — the man was an earl — Amelia respected his wish to remain anonymous and returned his smile. "Fear not, my lord. I do not intend to stand on ceremony while at a coaching inn. Come, let us get Cate bathed, then mayhap the three of us might partake of a meal without worrying about convention."

She held his gaze, and he found himself agreeing, even though he realised it was bordering on the improper.

Amelia took pity on him, adding, "Do not fret, I am a widow—" She broke off when Ruby appeared to tell them the bath was ready.

Taking Cate's hand, Amelia followed Lord Badlesmere up

the stairs and along the gallery to the opposite end of the same floor on which her own room was situated.

Once she had unlocked the door, Ruby tucked the key, which hung off a huge ring, back under her apron, and stood aside to let them in.

"Thank you, Ruby, and please, would you add two more meals to mine to be served in about an hour?" Amelia made her request politely.

Ruby nodded and scurried off, plenty of other things to keep her occupied.

In the middle of the room, one much larger than hers, Amelia spied a copper tub, steam hovering above it. Cate rushed over, leant in and sniffed purposefully, then turned to Amelia, her mouth drooping.

"What's wrong, dear?" Amelia asked.

"It doesn't smell pretty." Cate pouted.

Amelia swallowed a grin. "Give me a moment."

She hurried out of the room and along to her own chambers. From inside her valise, she plucked the tiny bottle of lavender water used to keep her clothes fresh. It would do the trick. Retracing her steps, she knocked and re-entered the room.

"Add a few drops of this." She removed the stopper from the vial and handed it to Cate.

Cate lifted the bottle to her nose and drew a gentle breath, a beam lighting up her face. "Oh, this is the prettiest smell." She shook the bottle vigorously over the water.

Amelia caught the child's hand before too much went in and became overwhelming. The light fragrance permeated the room, making it feel cleaner somehow.

"Come on then, young lady, shall we get you out of these clothes?" Once Cate was undressed, Amelia — recalling something her nanny used to do when she was a child —

tested the water with her elbow. In spite of the steam, it wasn't too hot, and she lifted Cate in.

The child sank into the tub with more enthusiasm than grace, splattering water everywhere.

"Cate, please do not drench Mrs Danneville. She is being kind enough to bath you. *Do* try not to be such a heathen," Rupert scolded.

Cate looked at Amelia and, not in the slightest contrite, chuckled. About to splash her hand into the water, she spotted a warning glint in Amelia's eyes.

Amelia shook her head. "I am happy for you to play a little, but please do not soak me intentionally. I would have to change, which is unfair when you begged me to help, don't you think?"

While Cate considered this, Amelia added. "If you behave, I shall wash your hair, then you can dry it in front of this lovely fire, and you will understand why I like baths." She raised an eyebrow, "Do we have a bargain?"

Cate glanced at her father.

Out of the corner of her eye, Amelia saw him nod.

"We do," Cate agreed.

"Shake on it," Amelia said, putting out her hand. "This is how adults seal a pact," she clarified in secretive tones.

Cate giggled and shook hands. Accord reached, Amelia sponged her down thoroughly, ensuring every last smear of mud was removed. The tub was duly refilled with fresh water, and Amelia washed Cate's hair, plucking all manner of detritus from the dark locks in the process.

Satisfied, Amelia wrapped the child in a large, linen drying sheet, and carried her over to the chair by the fire. After towelling her dry, she helped the sleepy girl into the nightdress and robe her father had laid out.

While Cate got herself settled herself in front of the fire, Amelia took a few moments to rinse out the mud-encrusted stockings. When they, finally, came clean, she hung them over the back of a chair to dry overnight.

Turning her attention to Cate's hair, Amelia rubbed the curly mop rigorously in the damp sheet, and by now, it was all the little girl could do to stay upright. The warmth of the bath, the heat from the crackling fire, and a long day in the fresh air — not to mention several temper tantrums — had exhausted her.

"I think you might want to ask Ruby to bring your food up here. Cate is almost asleep." Amelia spoke quietly, surprised by an unexpected rush of sadness at not being able to share a meal with this taciturn gentleman. She dismissed it, as Rupert nodded and left the room. Lifting a drowsy Cate onto her lap, Amelia concentrated on brushing the little girl's dark locks until they shone.

Cate yawned, snuggling into Amelia, little hands slipping around her waist. Without thinking, Amelia began to croon a lullaby.

His request made for all three meals to be served in his chamber — studiously disregarding how the arrangement might appear — Rupert Latimer entered the room to an attractive scene.

His daughter, her little face slightly flushed from the bath, was fast asleep with her dark head tucked under Amelia's chin. Amelia was absently stroking one hand over the child's hair and down her back while she sang.

Her sweet voice brought a tranquillity to the room and, if he was honest, himself.

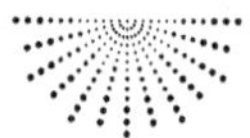

ransfixed, Rupert wished Cate had a mother who sang her to sleep every night. The oddest notion that Mrs Danneville would fit the role admirably, flittered through his subconscious. It was gone before he could capture it but left him mildly unsettled.

He moved towards her, the floorboards creaking to announce his approach.

Amelia turned her head and smiled.

"Apparently, I am a comfortable cushion," she murmured in undertones.

Rupert lifted his daughter out of Amelia's arms, and laid her gently on the small cot at the far end of the chamber. He covered her with the quilt, waiting until sure she was not going to wake.

"I have asked Ruby to send your meal here if that is not too impertinent. I did not feel it polite to expect you to eat alone after all you have done."

"I have done nothing but thank you for your kindness. It will make a change to have some company while dining."

Amelia grinned engagingly as Ruby appeared with two bowls of delicious-smelling stew.

A few moments of awkward silence ensued until Amelia, used to putting people at ease, asked Rupert an innocuous question and they began a comfortable conversation.

"What brings you to Cirencester? If I may be so bold as to ask?" Rupert said as they finished their meal.

"I was possessed with a yearning to spend some time on my own following the death of my husband," she replied. "I have seen little of what lies beyond the confines of London and was possessed with an ardent desire to explore some of it. Being a widow affords me some freedom, so 'tis just my driver and myself."

She went on to tell him which places she wanted to visit and why, astounding herself. She was normally far more reticent.

Rupert listened attentively, regarding Amelia, unobtrusively. At first glance, she looked unprepossessing, but he realised this was contrived rather than natural. Taller than most women of his acquaintance, Amelia was fair of skin, with a smattering of freckles sprinkled across her pert nose.

Her hair was dark-blonde, but even though constrained in an unflattering style, the glow from the candles picked out golden highlights. Her eyes were an odd shade. Hazel, Rupert thought might be the correct descriptor, but as Amelia chatted, the colour seemed to vary with her emotions. In fact, he found himself captivated by them.

As their conversation went back and forth, Amelia seized the opportunity to survey Rupert, although she would not call him that to his face. He was a good head taller than she, which to Amelia was unusual, being roughly the same height as the majority of gentlemen she knew.

His hair was almost black, but she discerned a hint of grey at his temples, making his age difficult to guess, not that she had any reason to. The mere idea bringing a slight flush to her cheeks. His eyes, like Cate's, were grey, but not cold, and they twinkled when he smiled which, she noted, was infrequently.

Rupert was darkly arresting. While his rugged good-looks might not be considered fashionably attractive by the current crop of debutantes, to Amelia, he exuded a charisma, which was far too appealing for his, *or her*, own good.

Unnerved by her reaction to this man who remained, in essence, a stranger, she broke off in the middle of a sentence. Thanking him for his hospitality, adding her hope that he and Cate found the remainder of their stay agreeable — Amelia fled.

Rupert Latimer, Earl of Badlesmere, watched her go. A slight smile tugged at his lips, and his heart responded to an emotion his head could not define.

It was mid-afternoon. Amelia, swallowing her customary disinclination to ride had, to her own surprise, enjoyed her day. Hiring a placid mare named Lottie, she had trotted down leafy lanes, and galloped across open countryside, relishing the freedom.

Lunch, a delicious picnic packed by Ruby, had been eaten while sitting on a wall, to the inquisitive astonishment of a herd of cows. A wholly unladylike, yet wholly pleasurable pastime.

Coming to the end of a dusty track on the outskirts of Cirencester, Amelia was about to point Lottie in the direction of her accommodation when a familiar shriek rang out. Turning in the saddle, she spied an open-topped carriage rolling into view along the narrow road.

"Mrs Dandelion, Mrs Dandelion. Papa, look who it is."

Cate's clarion tones shattered the peace of the afternoon, and the child's continued mispronunciation of her name, made Amelia grin. Tilting her bonnet to keep the sun out of her eyes, Amelia held Lottie steady while they approached.

Cate was jumping up and down in glee. Rupert's demeanour was less austere than appeared to be his habit, and he held Amelia's gaze for seconds longer than necessary when they came to a halt alongside her.

"Mrs Dandelion, what are you doing here?" Cate's piping question dragged Amelia's attention away from those smoky eyes, which did peculiar things to her insides.

"I have been exploring this beautiful countryside," she replied. "Where are you two going on so glorious an afternoon?"

"We are going for an ice. Papa says it's because I was a good girl this morning."

"I had to see a man about some business. To leave Cate unattended at the inn was unthinkable, the only alternative, to take her with me. She behaved like an angel, waiting quietly until our discussion was concluded. To my amazement," Rupert felt impelled to clarify.

Amelia smiled at the little girl. "That sounds quite lovely, and 'tis the nicest reward."

"Papa, might Mrs Dandelion come with us?" Cate asked, giving her father little choice in the matter.

Amelia started to splutter excuses. They didn't know her

at all…. and it was a treat and… Whatever else she tried to say was lost when Cate stretched out of the carriage to catch Amelia's hands.

"Mrs Dandelion," she spoke seriously. "You bathed me last night so this can be your treat too." Cate smiled beatifically.

Amelia found herself agreeing even though she probably should not. It was unfair to become friendly with Cate, only to walk out of her life.

"I believe I am persuaded and would be glad to join you. This was a special treat from your father to you, however, and first you should have asked him whether he minded you inviting me." Amelia's gentle smile took any censure from her words.

Cate screwed up her face and glowered at Rupert, daring him to refuse her request.

"Please may she come with us, Papa?" Her plea was nothing short of grudging.

Rupert pretended to think about it, making Cate fidget. Her little hands twisted in her lap as she tried to contain herself.

He let several seconds tick by, before taking pity on his daughter. "I think that would be delightful," he replied, prompting Cate to jiggle around even more. Her excitement contagious.

Amelia gave up worrying and nudged Lottie forward onto the main road. The short ride to Cirencester was uneventful. As they reached the outskirts of town, Amelia spotted a tearoom, which also sold ices. Dismounting, she looped the mare's reins over a conveniently placed hitching post.

Brushing out her skirts, and patting her hair, hoping she looked presentable, Amelia entered the establishment, to see Rupert and Cate already ensconced at a table tucked into the bay window.

"Cate's choice." Rupert felt moved to explain.

"The perfect spot." Amelia's beam of approval, mirrored Cate's.

♨

Time ticked by pleasantly. The ices were declared to be the tastiest *ever*, and Cate chattered nineteen to the dozen about goodness knew what. Her ability to change the subject without warning, left Amelia gasping.

Rupert did not say much. He was content to observe, curious about Amelia's determination to appear as unremarkable as possible.

As the afternoon drew to a close, and Amelia rose from the table to take her leave.

"Thank you, Cate and Lord Badlesmere," she said quietly. "This has been delightful. Mayhap I shall see you before I depart The Lion and Eagle."

"Where are you going?" Cate demanded.

"To continue my travels. To stay at the coaching inn indefinitely, is not suitable. I only planned to break my journey here, two nights at most."

Cate's lips began to wobble. "You cannot leave." Her voice was husky, and her eyes glimmered with unshed tears.

"Sweetheart, Miss Danneville has things to d—"

Before Rupert could say anymore, Cate screwed up her face and released an ear-splitting scream.

"**Noooooooooooooooo**."

Mortified as well as furious, Rupert reached for his daughter. She would have none of it and, hurling herself off the chair, clung to Amelia's legs.

. . .

Amelia was unperturbed by this overly dramatic display. Her lack of experience with children — small or otherwise — notwithstanding, instinct took over. Lifting Cate into her arms, Amelia carried her outside the tearoom, rocked the little girl for a moment or two, then stood her on the ground.

Cate sobbed wretchedly, her reaction far outweighing the situation.

Rupert followed them out, his lips pressed together in a flat line. Amelia could see he was about to upbraid his daughter. Somewhere in the back of her mind, she knew this would only make things worse.

Before he had a chance to speak, Amelia knelt next to Cate and cupped her little face.

"Cate."

Cate offered no response, just noisy sobs.

"Cate," Amelia repeated briskly.

Cate hiccuped and, shoving her thumb in her mouth, looked at Amelia. Her dove grey eyes, so like her father's, swimming with tears.

"Cate my precious, what brought this on? Surely you knew we would have to say goodbye?"

Cate scrubbed at her face. "I w-wanted you to s-stay," she blubbered. "Everyone always l-leaves me."

The child's disconsolate tones nearly undid Amelia, and she had no idea how to console her. Hugging her close, she glanced up at Rupert who was regarding the two of them, his countenance unreadable.

Amelia stood and stroked her fingers through Cate's curly hair in a comforting gesture.

"Please do not be angry with her, Lord Latimer. I do believe she is simply exhibiting feelings of abandonment. No, not from you..." she said quickly, when he began to splutter a response. "Both you and Cate told me every nanny has left her, and presumably, she either never knew or knew her mother only briefly?"

She arched a quizzical eyebrow, and Rupert nodded slowly.

"Then, we met yesterday and, although we have shared but a few hours of fun, I am about to do the same. As adults, you and I understand people come and go in our lives, sometimes without explanation. The minds of young children have not developed enough to process it in the same way, and it manifests like grief. People keep coming into her life, spend time with her, maybe spoil her, and then disappear. I think Cate feels to blame."

"She hasn't exactly behaved in a manner that might encourage people to stay. Cate is obdurate, bossy, demanding, temperamental, and more than a little overindulged." Rupert admitted ruefully, ire at his daughter's behaviour churning.

"Of course, she is. She requires boundaries and limits. Someone to explain there are consequences for her actions and not be afraid to mete out punishment if she breaks the rules. Nothing harsh, just something, which will give her pause should she think of repeating it.

"Cate is a small child, my lord, she needs to know how far she can push, and if no one stops her, she will keep pushing. Trust me, it will build upon, not destroy, your bond."

Amelia took a deep breath, concerned she had overstepped her own boundaries. As the widow of an earl, her observations would not be perceived as impertinent, but Rupert did not know her status. To him, she was just some woman dishing out — probably unwanted — advice about his daughter.

Rupert was staring at her, his brow lowered.

"I beg your pardon." She sketched a curtsy. "It was not my

intent to interfere. My mother was always quick to remonstrate when my mouth ran away with me."

Before he could respond, Amelia turned her attention to Cate. "Cate, sweetheart, how about we stretch our legs and let your papa have a moment to himself."

Without waiting for permission from Rupert, she held out her hand until she felt Cate's hot and sticky little paw grasp it, and the two swung out along the path.

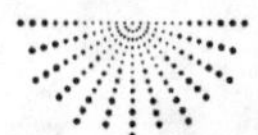

CHAPTER FIVE

Rupert Latimer stood motionless, while he tried to come to grips with what Amelia had said. She was right, but his time with Cate was fleeting. His days were spent attending business of one form or another, and by mid-evening when, finally, he had some free time, Cate was usually in bed.

His daughter required a firmer hand, but he couldn't bring himself to do it. While mulling this over, the same notion which had popped into his head the previous afternoon, came back to him. The more he thought about it, the more it offered the perfect solution. His only problem was convincing Amelia.

A few steps behind, Rupert listened to his daughter's garrulous chatter as she skipped rather than walked next to Amelia. He was intrigued by this woman. Outwardly composed, she could break into spontaneous bouts of laughter.

He knew nothing about her, except her bearing was of someone who had spent hours learning deportment. Her skin was clear and soft, and her hands not calloused. She was certainly not a member of the working class.

Who was Mrs Amelia Danneville, and why was she travelling incognito? Yes, she was a conundrum. Maybe his suggestion might prompt her to be more forthcoming.

Although why he needed her to, he had yet to fathom.

Catching up easily with his long, loping stride, Rupert added his voice to their chatter. Cate's outburst was not forgotten necessarily but pushed to the back of their minds for the time being. They meandered along the River Churn for a little way, Cate stopping to throw the odd pebble into the water.

Rupert demonstrated how to skim flat ones across the water. Cate desperately tried to copy him, finally getting one to skip twice, to her own elation and rapturous applause from her modest audience.

Contemplating their interaction, it was clear to Amelia that Rupert loved his daughter but was perhaps overwhelmed by the responsibilities of being a parent.

Even though Amelia realised Cate's behaviour was her way of getting his attention, if allowed to continue, both would suffer.

They meandered back to the tearoom where the coach and Lottie awaited. Amelia thanked the two for a lovely afternoon, agreeing, after more pleas from Cate, to join them for the evening meal.

Once in the saddle, Amelia waved, wheeled the horse around, and trotted off, her mind whirling. Unrecognisable emotions were clouding her senses. Rupert was dangerously handsome which, along with his grave disposition and quick wit, made him an intriguing man, but what of it?

She was recently widowed, scarcely six weeks ago, and he was simply a gentleman she met by accident. Anything beyond that could not be contemplated. Soon, she would depart, and that would be that, leaving naught but the memory of an entertaining interlude.

Infusing practicality into the situation, Amelia contrived to dispatch any and all thoughts teasing at her to the far recesses of her mind, determined not to read anything into them.

Bowing to the inevitable, Amelia extended her stay at the inn for two more nights. She hoped this might lessen Cate's misery, taking pains to clarify her departure could not be delayed beyond the end of the week.

The three explored more of the city and its surroundings, had their meals together, and generally had a marvellous time.

Even though she savoured this sojourn with the Latimers, Amelia knew she had to leave before it became too hard. Without trying, Cate was already too close to her heart.

Moreover, Rupert's behaviour was downright confusing.

With her, he was polite and a little standoffish. This was to be expected. They didn't know each other.

With Cate he was either remote and unyielding or overindulgent, and it exasperated Amelia. If she spent too long in his company, she might be tempted to slap some sense into him. Not the most judicious idea.

§

Amelia's last day was spent pottering about before walking down to the River Churn for a picnic. Cate had fun paddling, in her bare feet this time, so as not to ruin another pair of shoes and stockings.

The simple joy at being allowed to play unencumbered by the usual constraints was evidenced in the little girl's unbridled enthusiasm, her lively antics reducing her father and Amelia to gales of laughter.

Tomorrow Amelia would depart and, although excited about exploring new pastures, she experienced a curious ache. One she ignored, instead concentrating on what to wear. Staring at the gowns hanging in the excuse for a wardrobe, she frowned.

Her options were grey, darker grey, or grey. While it had been her decision to adhere to the conventions of mourning, she was heartily sick of the dowdy colour. *Why had she not chosen some of the richer greys, those which appeared to be blended with purple or blue or even dark red?* The flat shade she had ended up with leached all the life out of her face.

Nevertheless, they were all she had, so she shrugged into one. The multitude of buttons, normally fastened by a maid, no longer a hindrance.

§

Curled up on Amelia's lap, Cate played with her new favourite person's string of pearls, while the two adults sipped a tankard of beer each.

Amelia had developed a partiality for the amber liquid. It was refreshing at the end of a long day and less heady than wine or spirits. She was careful to restrict herself to one serving, aware how easily she might become tipsy.

Rupert had been quiet this evening, letting Cate dictate the chatter.

His reserve had not gone unnoticed by Amelia. It was not her place to question it, but she confessed to feeling a trifle dismayed. She thought they had reached a kind of equanimity. More at ease with each other than when first they met.

She had not reproached him. Not once, despite the several instances when she wanted to yell and scream at him for being so blinkered where Cate was concerned. *Was it too much to ask he act as though he might miss her, even if he would not?*

It was noisy in the parlour. The raucous behaviour of the locals and other guests in the adjoining bar was increasing in direct proportion to the amount of alcohol they consumed. Not a particularly conducive setting for private discussions anyway.

Cate was nodding off and, wearied of attempting to engage Rupert in conversation, Amelia decided it was high time she returned to her chambers.

She sighed heavily, causing Cate to shift sleepily in her arms and snuggle closer. Her chest tightened with unfamiliar emotions.

She had to stop this nonsense.

"Lord Badlesmere, thank you for yet another lovely evening. 'Tis time I retired. I have an early start, and there are various things I need to finalise with my packing." Her voice sounded hollow, but she couldn't help it.

She started to get up, only to be forestalled by Rupert's next words.

"Please, might you grant me a moment longer?"

Vacillating, briefly, Amelia sank back into the chair, Cate in her arms, and waited.

"As Cate is dozing, and therefore no longer privy to our conversation, I wonder whether you would be prepared to listen to a proposition? One to which I hope you might be amenable."

Amelia eyed him warily.

He raised his palms. "Nothing untoward, I promise."

"You may certainly make your proposition. Whether I accept has yet to be determined." She smiled slightly but could not shake the notion that what he was about to say would upend her life.

Rupert studied Amelia, carefully. Her guarded expression smoothed to bland and apparently uninterested, but he sensed a tension lurking.

He really wanted this to work.

Cate needed this to work.

Steeling himself, he plunged in.

"Mrs Danneville, these last few days have brought home to me the necessity for Cate to have a steadying and stable influence in her life. I have tried to be thus, but as previously noted, I do not have the luxury of devoting to my daughter the time she needs, and she has run off every nanny. Even members of my household have been known to avoid her unless they have no choice. I love my daughter, but I do not know where to turn or what to do."

He paused.

"Would you consider becoming her governess?"

CHAPTER SIX

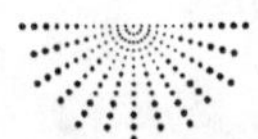

*W*hatever Amelia presumed Rupert had been going to suggest, this was so far in the opposite direction as to be coming back the other way. She stared at him, temporarily robbed of speech.

"W-what… but… w-why… m-must." Confounded, Amelia stopped trying to form a sentence. Taking a moment to coerce her thoughts into some semblance of order, she made a second attempt.

"I beg your pardon?"

Nonplussed, Amelia's eyes widened, and their tawny depths mesmerised Rupert.

How did one stop oneself from falling to another's gaze? No, that was not what he was supposed to be thinking about.

He repeated his question, elaborating somewhat on why he thought Amelia would be the perfect choice.

"You said yourself you are widowed and looking for a

little time away from the humdrum, the mundanity. Mayhap this affords you something of that. Badlesmere, my home, is quite large and borders on magnificent countryside. You could quench your thirst for exploring a corner of England while at the same time tutoring my daughter. You would, of course, be paid handsomely for your trouble." He concluded, staring at her optimistically.

Amelia bit her lip. She had no urgent need of money, but any extra would certainly help the Gresham coffers. It could go towards those repairs, delayed due to lack of ready funds. The little profit she had managed to procure during the last two years was apportioned among her staff and estate work-ers. Without them, Gresham Park would certainly have fallen into bankruptcy.

Rupert's offer was enticing.

Could she keep up the pretence?

"While your offer sounds appealing, I am compelled to ask, why me? You do not know me. What gives you the impression I would be a good influence on Cate? I might be akin to a witch in a folktale. Befriending you to steal away your daughter and sell her into slavery or worse, cook her in a pie."

Her last comment was a bid to get Rupert to smile. He was always so solemn.

Her bald declaration horrified Rupert and caused him, momentarily, to question his sanity. *What the devil was he thinking?* He wasn't addled enough to think she would eat his daughter… although… **no,** it definitely wasn't that, but Amelia was correct. He had not once considered she might have an ulterior motive.

His idea, which he believed to be timely, now seemed preposterous. Racking his brain for a polite way to rescind his offer, he caught sight of Amelia's mischievous grin, at variance with her words.

"You spoke in jest!" The relief on his face was comical.

"Of course. I much prefer little boys in my pies," she replied tartly but with a wicked chuckle.

He relaxed suddenly and, to Amelia's gratification, joined in her laughter.

"If you are prepared to look past my penchant for eating children, I should be honoured to take the position of governess to Cate," she said, disregarding the vague agreement she had made with her father-in-law not six weeks past.

Rupert called for another flagon of beer, and refilled both of their tankards. Ignoring an increasing light-headedness, Amelia accepted the top up. This was a celebration of sorts. Moreover, she deemed it churlish to refuse.

Cate hadn't stirred during their conversation, and Amelia, resting her chin on the child's curly hair, absently stroked up and down her arm. A wave of happiness washed over her at the thought of spending more time with this little girl whose chubby fingers were clutching more than her dress.

That it also meant she might come to know Rupert a little better was neither here nor there.

Badlesmere ~ June 1816

Two carriages rumbled down a lengthy driveway. It was late afternoon, and their journey from Cirencester had taken three days. The clouds hung low, but the forecast rain had held off, to no small relief of the passengers.

Cate had begged to be allowed to sit with Amelia for this last leg. Currently, she was leaning out of the window, calling out to a handful of estate workers who paused and waved to their diminutive mistress.

As the coaches crunched to a standstill in front of the imposing entrance, staff rushed to assist the travellers.

Cate jumped down and hopped around excitedly, generally getting under everyone's feet until Rupert suggested she might like to go and check whether the Willow Room would be suitable for Mrs Danneville.

That did the trick. She shot off into the house and, at Rupert's behest, a couple of maids bustled on her heels.

"Welcome to Badlesmere." Unthinking, Rupert offered Amelia his arm.

She hesitated. It was not done for an earl to offer his arm to a mere governess. Their previous acquaintance aside, not to mention her true status, Amelia did not want the household to think she was usurping her very new position.

He turned, raking hooded eyes over her while she dithered.

"'Tis unseemly, Lord Latimer," she murmured, a pink stain colouring her cheeks.

Rupert gaped, and his arm dropped to his side. "'Pon my word, what nonsense. You might be Cate's governess, but you are also a guest in my home. Not to mention, we have spent some part of every day together for the last week," he said, puzzled by her diffidence.

"Nevertheless, I think we ought to start as we shall go on."

She forced aside the overwhelming urge to clasp her fingers over the fine wool of his dark blue jacket.

Rupert shrugged. His genial manner morphed to sombre, but he said no more other than to ask her to accompany him.

Amelia was about to do so when she paused, entranced by the beauty of Badlesmere.

Built from the local, aged, pale-gold Bath stone, the Elizabethan mansion appeared to float in a sea of lush lawns and colourful flowerbeds.

The towering central section was softened by symmetrical wings on either side and punctuated by gables and windows — so many windows — under a roofline littered with chimneys, parapets and balustrades.

To Amelia, the bookworm, it was evocative of the medieval chivalric tales she loved to read. Tales of castles and knights and maidens. Gresham Park was lovely but, compared with Badlesmere, relatively new and very much lacking in architectural imagination.

Engrossed in her admiration, Amelia lost her sense of place. A not-so-subtle cough brought her back to earth.

"I do beg your pardon, my lord. It's just… your home is enchanting." She beamed at Rupert, his brusque manner forgotten, her whole face lighting up, causing him to blink and swallow twice before he was able to speak with any coherence.

"I am glad it meets with your approval," Rupert was unable to prevent a hint of sarcasm in his tone, only to feel like a cad when he saw Amelia's smile fade.

Remembering her position, Amelia dipped a curtsey. "Thank you for allowing me to take a moment. I imagine you have things to which you must attend, and it was not my intent to delay you. Pray, do not worry about me. I daresay one of your lovely staff will show me to the domestic quarters." She schooled her features and tempered her enthusiasm.

"You shall not be residing in the servants' wing, Mrs Danneville. Your chambers are in the main house." Again, he had no intention of being abrupt, but it was too late. Rupert tutted under his breath and pivoted on his heel. "Please, come with me." He stalked purposefully through the front door.

Dubiously, Amelia traipsed behind. He was behaving like a bear with a sore paw. *Was this a huge mistake? Yes, their time at Cirencester had been congenial but surely, he realised their relationship had shifted. He was no longer an acquaintance. He was her employer.* Amelia was flummoxed and, even accepting she would be taking orders instead of giving them, this was outside her experience.

She did not know how to react.

In the cosy parlour of a coaching inn, what had sounded like an interesting way to discover more of the countryside — while teaching a child all she would need to know as the daughter of an earl — now seemed foolish in the extreme.

Too late my girl, she admonished herself. *You agreed to do this. Now straighten your shoulders and get on with it. What did you think? That Rupert's slow thawing would continue? Gracious me, get your head out of the clouds.*

Duly chastised, she followed her own instructions and wiped her face of all expression save one of bland politeness.

Upon reaching the second floor of the central section of the house, Rupert stopped outside an open door just off the wide landing.

"These are your quarters. Forster will bring your luggage, and Lilly will be your assigned maid. Dinner will be served at seven. I trust you will join us?" His tones were clipped.

Amelia dipped another curtsy. "Thank you, Lord Badlesmere, that sounds quite agreeable. Might I be permitted to take a short stroll in the gardens beforehand? It has been a long day in a carriage, and I feel the need to stretch my legs." She held his gaze, but her eyes no longer sparkled, and her voice had lost its lilt.

Whatever had begun to grow between them, even if it were merely friendship, was slipping away.

Rupert frowned. "You do not need to ask, Mrs Danneville. This is now your home, and I trust you will treat it as such. The grounds are yours to explore at your leisure, and I suspect Cate will be eager to show you around."

Disconcerted by Amelia's stiff bearing, Rupert speculated as to the reason. Nothing came to him. He bowed and disappeared down the stairs, calling that he would see her later.

Leaning on the doorjamb, Amelia watched him go, then shook herself and turned to inspect her new abode. The room was spectacular, decorated in soft green hues, reminiscent of the first flush of spring. Positioned between two of the windows, a sumptuous looking bed, its layers of quilts, most inviting.

Amelia stroked her hand over the luxurious material, hearing it crinkle under her fingertips. A small square cabinet was tucked in next to the head of the bed, atop which had been placed a candle, a goblet, and a jug of cool water.

Opposite the bed, all but filling the wall, a fireplace — laid but not lit — circled by two delicately carved chairs. To the right, a dressing room — complete with armoire, dressing table, two more chairs and another large window.

Amelia stood for several moments, admiring its elegant simplicity.

Going to the window closest to her, she flung it open,

inhaling the slightly damp air, and taking in the magnificent view.

She surmised this room must be at the back of Badlesmere, for she did not recall passing so vast a swathe of trees on their approach to the house. Gentle woodland becoming dark forest and stretching as far as the eye could see.

Walking around the bed, Amelia unlatched the window at that side too. Leaning on the frame, she lingered, letting her thoughts roam as the late afternoon breeze freshened the room.

Inexplicably, she felt at home.

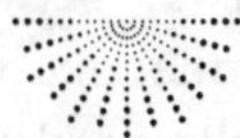

CHAPTER SEVEN

Unsure when her luggage would be brought up, Amelia freshened up in the bowl provided before retracing her steps.

Her hand smoothed over the cool polished oak of the balustrade as she descended the curved staircase, and she drank in the beauty of the entrance hall.

About to step outside, her progress was halted by a loud yell.

"Mrs Dandelion, Mrs Dandelion, wait for me. I want to come too." Cate hurtled down the stairs and into Amelia's arms. "I *am* glad you're here. What do you want to see first?"

Prattling away merrily, Cate towed Amelia down the steps and around to the left-hand side of the mansion, past one of the wings.

Amelia took the liberty of glancing in through a few windows, spotting a large ballroom and several smaller rooms, prompting her to speculate where she would hold Cate's lessons.

She was given no further chance to ponder this because Cate was pointing out all manner of things. The kitchen gardens, the orchards, the walled garden, the stables, the workshops, and then out onto the expansive lawns at the rear of the property, which extended to the trees Amelia had spied from her window.

Water from three ornate fountains, standing proudly just off the broad terrace, flowed into shallow canals, each running into a lake halfway between the house and the woods. At the centre of the lake was an island on which nestled a Grecian-style folly, reached by a neat line of stepping-stones.

Amelia was captivated. *Definitely something out of a fury tale.* She had seen her fair share of ancestral homes and estates of the nobility, but nothing compared with this. The refined gentility combined with interesting quirks gave Badlesmere an inviting aspect despite its magnitude.

Beset by an irrational desire to remove her boots and stockings and run through the abundant grass, barefoot, Amelia sank to the ground. Arguing with herself that there was plenty of time to change before dinner, she gave in to temptation.

Cate watched fascinated, clapping with glee when she realised what Amelia was doing,

"May I also?" she pleaded.

"Of course. Come, let me help you." Amelia offered, uncaring what Rupert might think of this, her first act as governess. She folded their stockings and inserted each pair into their respective boots. Amelia tucked up the hem of her gown and then held out her hand to Cate, the two ambling down the gentle slope until they were on flatter ground.

Before Cate had time to question what they were going to do next, Amelia cried, "Catch me if you can," and sprinted off.

Not too quickly, just fast enough so Cate had to chase her.

The little girl flew across the lawn, screeching for her to wait.

Amelia stopped, turned, and whisked the child into her arms, swinging her around and around.

Laughter filled the air, disturbing Rupert who was going over an accumulation of papers in his study. Presuming the racket to be caused by unruly stable hands or the gardener's lads, he yanked open the French doors and took one step onto the terrace, ready to castigate the rascals.

His jaw dropped in shock when he spotted his daughter and her brand-new governess dancing about the grass with nothing on their feet. His first instinct was to rebuke both — Amelia for her juvenile behaviour and Cate for ignoring his rules about shoes and stockings.

Something made him pause.

Amelia was singing a nonsensical ditty, something about lavender, and Cate was jumping over goodness knows what, grass stalks probably. Their exhilaration in so simple a game brought a smile to his lips. *What was the harm?* Disinclined to ruin their fun, Rupert left them to it.

The days fell into an easy routine.

Each morning, after breakfast, Amelia helped her charge understand the basics. Cate was only four, and Amelia decided elementary reading, writing and addition was enough of a challenge for now. In the afternoons they explored the estate and, eventually, the surrounding countryside.

Mindful Cate was unaccustomed to rules of any kind, Amelia wrote out a rudimentary set, with which she expected the little girl to comply. Any breach resulted in a penance, but treats and rewards were bestowed with equal swiftness, and there was always time for playing barefoot in the grass if Cate had tried her best.

At first it was a tussle, and Amelia was faced with numerous bouts of histrionics. She refused to give in and, slowly, Cate's tantrums were lessening. The little girl quickly recognised how far to push her governess, and when Amelia said 'enough', Cate knew that to goad her any further would have consequences.

A spirited child, Cate would never be the epitome of tranquillity, and Amelia had no mind to quash her exuberance, but she was learning how to curb her fiery temper. To ask when something didn't go her way, instead of ranting at all and sundry.

In her free time, Amelia made the effort to get to know Rupert's staff. By the end of her first fortnight, she knew everyone's names, making it her business to chat with as many as possible each day. They welcomed her good-naturedly and, before long, genuine friendship sprang up between them.

When Cate required an afternoon nap, Amelia ventured further afield, riding one of the estate horses. She loved these brief excursions. The wind in her hair, not a care in the world.

These snatched moments of uninhibited freedom, afforded Amelia ample time to contemplate her future. The six months were passing more quickly than she anticipated.

Unless Rupert was away, instead of eating in the nursery, Amelia and Cate dined with him. Their mealtime conversations covered a diverse range of topics and were often riotous.

The days became weeks, and Rupert's habitual gravity softened.

The more she got to know him, the more Amelia realised how much she liked him, discerning his gruff manner was a shield. A way of protecting himself. A barrier he never put between himself and his daughter, something about which Amelia had been concerned.

Determined to break through to the man underneath, she refused to let him retreat into his shell as he seemed predisposed to do when another got too close. By including him in some of their activities, she got him to open up about Cate and by extension himself. Purely for Cate's benefit, of course.

Rupert looked forward to the banter they shared, relishing their lively debates. It wasn't long before he began listening to Amelia's opinion on various matters. Initially, their conversations centred around Cate, but soon, and almost without realising it, Rupert was seeking Amelia's advice on almost every aspect of his life. He appreciated her sharp mind and intuitive grasp of the management of vast estates.

Her knowledge of the latter piqued his curiosity, not entirely convinced by the hurried explanation that her uncle was chief steward on the estate of some minor noble.

Amelia was hiding something, and he meant to get to the bottom of it.

Uncertain what it was about this self-possessed young woman, whose face was constantly in his thoughts, Rupert encouraged her to reveal something of her life before they met.

Amelia was as honest as possible in her answers, unwilling to admit her secret for fear it might fracture the fragile and virtually imperceptible accord blossoming between them.

At the same time — again persuading herself it was because of Cate — Amelia discovered all she could about Teresa Latimer. The name of the child's mother rang a distant bell, but she couldn't recall why, probably because she had spent the previous two years at Gresham Park, avoiding the gossip and innuendo so loved by Society. While, in some respects this was a blessing, it also meant Amelia had missed out on the idle chit chat where one was guaranteed to garner useful information.

Taking care not to appear overly inquisitive, she managed to wheedle snippets of information out of Lilly and some of the other staff. Artlessly asked questions engendered a plethora of answers, and weeding through the tittle-tattle, she eventually came to what she believed might be the truth.

Amelia's heart ached for Rupert. His dead wife sounded like a cold woman. An arranged marriage, no love lost on either side; consummated because it was expected. Instead of making the best of it, once increasing, Teresa had refused to share a bedchamber with her husband.

Immediately following Cate's birth, she had abandoned her tiny daughter to the care of a wet nurse and returned to London. Rumoured to have indulged in several scandalous affairs, Teresa Latimer succumbed to a fever a year later, without ever seeing her daughter again.

Oddly, although Hayward and Amelia had never shared a bed, the story bore echoes of her own marriage. Both arranged, neither caring for each other, and one dying unexpectedly. The difference being, in one there was a child.

Lack of affection had stifled Amelia's dream of being a mother, along with any hope of love. Now, she was responsible for the well-being of a child she cared for as though her own, and whose father had somehow kindled a flame she presumed impossible to ignite.

CHAPTER EIGHT

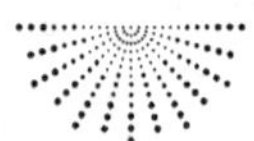

*P*rior to leaving Cirencester, Amelia had dispatched a letter to Mr Williams apprising him of her temporary address and requesting he keep her whereabouts private, unless absolutely essential.

In turn, he briefed her regularly on Gresham Park, and Amelia was gratified to note her steward was managing the property efficiently.

Amelia had also asked the kindly solicitor to arrange for one of her staff to send more clothes and was delighted when a large trunk was delivered in early September. Per Amelia's detailed instructions, it contained gowns in a rainbow of hues.

She took wicked pleasure in shoving the detested greys into the trunk, which was then removed to one of the attics. Preferring to wear dresses of muted tones during the day, as befitted her current station, to have a choice of colourful gowns was a blessed relief.

In spite of Amelia's resolve to maintain her mediocre appearance, she was unaware her efforts were in vain. The earl observed her unwitting metamorphosis, with fascinated regularity.

When Amelia played with Cate or returned from a ride, her hair often unravelled from its tight bun. Shining curls falling around cheeks glowing from the fresh air. Amelia's bright smile, flashing eyes and cheerful demeanour, elicited emotions Rupert Latimer presumed long dead.

The weeks slid by. August blazed into September, then drifted quietly into October. The days shortened, an autumnal crispness cooling the last of the summer heat. Leaves changed, yellow, red, and purple replacing tired green, and the dazzling blue of the sky softened.

One morning, Amelia realised she had been at Badlesmere nearly four months.

A chill in the air had prompted Amelia to choose a light-wool day dress in a shade of dark bronze; a shawl, the colour of ginger biscuits, slung around her shoulders for extra warmth.

After a tasty breakfast, eaten in the warmth of the nursery, Amelia hustled Cate down to the small room set aside as a classroom. They had been absorbed in their lessons for about an hour when there was a knock at the door, and Lilly peeped in.

"His Lordship wants to see you in the study, miss. I'll stay with Cate while you go."

"Thank you, Lilly. I shall return as quickly as possible."

Wondering what on earth Rupert needed her for, Amelia ran her mind back over the last couple of weeks. Nothing stood out as being untoward, so she relaxed a little. Maybe he just wanted an update on Cate's progress.

Reaching the study, Amelia knocked on the door. She heard Rupert's muffled 'enter' and, taking a breath, stepped into the room. An elderly man, whom she did not recognise, stood by the fire, puffing on a pipe, the pungent aroma making her want to sneeze.

"You wish to see me, my lord?" she asked in carefully modulated tones, dropping the expected curtsy.

Amelia was unaware of the effect the whisper of her gown had on Rupert. The earl was acutely conscious, not only of how well the shade complemented her striking features, but also the adorable way in which her nose crinkled when she caught a whiff of the pipe smoke.

Yes, this could work.

"Mrs Danneville, may I introduce my solicitor, Mr Archibald?" he said, dragging his concentration back to the matter at hand.

Amelia smiled at the elderly gentleman and dipped her head. "Good morning, sir. A pleasure to meet you."

"The pleasure is all mine, Mrs Danneville," Mr Archibald replied affably, smoke curling around his whiskered face.

"Maybe you would like to sit?" Rupert invited.

Amelia eyed him. The earl's expression, while a tad grim, was inscrutable. Remembering her place, she sank into one the comfortable chairs near the fire, folded her hands on her lap, and waited.

The silence in the room lengthened.

Amelia started to feel like a stretched thread, on the verge of snapping.

"Firstly, I would like to apologise for what I am about to say. I had hoped to broach this… err… hmmm… delicate subject in a more leisurely fashion, but today, I received information, which precipitated my decision."

Amelia was baffled, but Rupert was still speaking.

"The family of my late wife are questioning my abilities as Cate's father, citing indifference to her welfare and general neglect." He held up a hand when Amelia started to splutter. "You, I hope, know differently, but Teresa's father is a marquis and may bring his position to bear in order to be granted guardianship of my daughter."

Unable to stay her tongue, Amelia burst out. "Lord Badlesmere, I have witnessed myself the love you bear for Cate and know her happiness and well-being take precedence over everything else. How could *anyone* accuse you of something so heinous? Surely they have no valid reason to challenge your competence as her father?"

Her voice rose as the ramifications of his words swept over her.

No. *No.* **No**!

To accuse Rupert of being an inadequate parent was utterly without merit.

Cate would be devastated, as would the man in front of her.

She was just a little girl. She had already lost so much. Now this.

Amelia got up from her chair, sat down, then stood and began to pace. Her distress far greater than was warranted from a lowly governess.

While Rupert did not wish to cause upset, Amelia's reaction gave him hope.

"This is where you might be able, once again, to help me."

"Me? Help? Whatever you need, my lord. Just tell me. Do you require a written declaration of how capable you are? Mayhap I should request an interview with the man," she said, forgetting her supposed status and that, as a governess, she would be considered an upstart for daring to propose such a thing.

Continuing to stride up and down the room, wringing her hands together, Amelia muttered about what she might do to prevent a catastrophe.

Amused by Amelia's tenacity, Rupert's heart swelled. His unanticipated affection for this woman had bloomed into something far deeper, and to him, her lack of status was irrelevant.

No one was more suited to be his wife and the mother of his child. Of course, he would have preferred to court her properly, but time was of the essence, and he could not lose Cate.

Would she be amenable?

He took a breath.

"Mrs Danneville."

She didn't hear him.

"Amelia!"

She stopped mid-stride and mid-mutter, spinning around to stare at him.

It was the first time he had called her Amelia. Was that significant?

"Amelia, thank you for your… interesting… suggestions, but I think I know a way to solve everything. A resolution if you will, which I trust might make us all happy."

She waited.

"I wonder whether you would consider becoming my wife?"

Amelia's jaw dropped. There was no other description for her stunned response. She started to respond, but her mind went blank. Marry him! ***Marry him?***

Gawking at Rupert, her manners quite thoughtlessly abandoning her, Amelia realised she had never wanted anything more in her entire life and, in that split second, acknowledged she was hopelessly in love with him. Unfortunately, her persona, and therefore her life here was a lie. He had no idea of her heritage, of her background.

Oh no, this could not be happening.

Her thoughts spun out as she raised her eyes to his.

Rupert flinched at the despair in her gaze.

"Amelia? What is it? My intent was not to offend. Surely you know I care for you. I believe we would muddle along nicely and perhaps, in time, you might have some affection for me. Moreover, I know how much you love Cate—"

"'Tis not that," Amelia interrupted before he went any further.

Care for her? Muddle along? Really?

It wasn't enough.

She didn't want him to *care* for her, even the word was insipid.

She wanted him to love her passionately, tenderly, unreservedly, and irrevocably.

Care for her.

It sounded as though she was a pet dog.

No, it sounded worse than her last marriage.

A spark of temper flared, and since it was likely she was about to ruin her carefully constructed façade anyway, she let it simmer.

"While I understand your motives, which are laudable, I am afraid I must decline." She thought she saw something resembling pain flicker across Rupert's face, masked before she could be certain.

"There are things about me of which you are unaware. In and of themselves they may not affect your... errr... offer, but the fact I have not been completely honest with you, might. I imagine you would prefer your wife to be above reproach."

· · ·

Rupert was now the one who tried to interrupt, but Amelia forged ahead, determined to reveal what she had taken great pains to disguise.

CHAPTER NINE

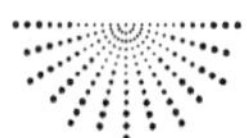

"My name is not Danneville. Well, it was before my marriage. I am, in fact, Lady Gresham, widow of Hayward Ingram, fourth Earl of Gresham, and now a countess in my own right. My father is the Marquis of Thetford.

"Following my husband's death which, by the way was, not from fever as was put about — he was killed in a stupid and unnecessary duel over gambling debts — I decided I needed six months away from everything.

"My father-in-law wanted me to marry Hayward's cousin, Ambrose, a man for whom I have even less affection than I had my own husband, and I did not think that was humanly possible.

"My whole life until that point had been dictated by someone else's whim, and I was weary of it. I informed them of my decision, allowing that at the end of the six months I might, potentially, consider Ambrose's suit."

Amelia's face contorted as she shuddered at the memory, prompting Rupert to take a step closer to her, but she wasn't finished.

Gathering herself, she held up her hand, palm facing him as though creating an invisible wall between them.

Rupert frowned. This wasn't how it was supposed to go.

"I must beg your forgiveness, my lord. Yes, I love Cate, but I accepted this position under false pretences. To help the pair of you to understand each other better. To work towards strengthening the close bond you already share. To assist Cate in her lessons. These last few months have been the most rewarding experience of my life, and I am truly grateful.

"My husband gambled away nearly all the Gresham monies. I believe I have managed to turn around my fortunes, but the generous wage you offered for my services was a boon I could not refuse."

Amelia wasn't really sure why she was telling him any of this. Her brain and her mouth had disconnected, and words tumbled over her lips in no particular order. Unbidden, tears began to form. She blinked them back and tried to clarify.

"Thank you for being so kind as to consider me suitable for the position of your wife." She tried to swallow on her growing ire.

Suitable. Dear lord, that was about as thrilling as being *cared* for.

Was she really so uninteresting, that the principal emotion anyone could conjure up about her was *suitable* or *nice?*

A wave of unutterable sadness fought with her anger, and even though she would always love Rupert, Amelia could not agree to a marriage where once more she would be ignored.

Not when this time her heart was at risk.

"Besides that, the reason I must decline is because to enter into another marriage lacking any devotion is unconscionable. My first marriage was barren. Neither of us had any measure of feeling for the other. I do not wish to be 'cared' for. I wish — no, I *deserve* to be loved and cherished. I need my husband to yearn for me, not once in a blue moon but every single day. I want him to think nothing of seeking me out at inopportune moments, to kiss me for no other reason than it is his ardent desire."

Amelia's temper spilled over.

"To be *cared* for is not and will never be enough. I have no desire to muddle along nicely. That smacks of disinterest. I want my marriage to be stimulating and challenging. I want to laugh, cry, argue, dance. Paddle in rivers, skim stones, eat ices, go on adventures. Then, when all is done, return to a home where my husband's embrace tells me I am the most loved woman on earth.

"Suitable…"

Incredulity lacing her tones, Amelia trailed off. She clutched her head, overwhelmed by the force of her emotions.

"Oh, God, I'm sorry," she spluttered and darted out of the French doors. She fled through the gardens and, coming to the lake, ran across the stepping-stones to the folly. Once there, she collapsed onto the stone bench, no longer able to stem the flood of tears.

Rupert and Mr Archibald stared at each other, speechless.

"I think you have your answer," ventured the solicitor after long moments of shocked silence. "Mind, she's a spirited one that. She'll keep you on your toes. I thought you said she was unassuming."

"She appeared thus, but it is curious, I have often wondered what would happen should she become infuriated, whether her reticence was inherent or by design. Amelia's manner with Cate is far less restrained than when she is in my presence.

"Now and again I have had the opportunity to watch their interaction, and 'tis a revelation. Amelia knows how to have fun, how to throw caution to the winds, how to laugh as though without a care in the world, to shed her genteel veneer, allowing her natural enthusiasm free rein.

"The first afternoon she was here, she encouraged Cate to run barefoot across the gardens, the two of them splashing in and out of the streams with carefree abandon. 'Tis only with me she is reserved. Now I know why. She has been acting a part, playing the dutiful governess.

"It also explains why she tried to make herself appear dowdy. How she actually acquired her exceptional knowledge of estate matters, and her awareness of the machinations within Society. I admit to being confused how someone outside the *ton* could gain such insights. Clever girl, Amelia."

Rupert tapped his chin, impressed with Amelia's keen intelligence and shrewd wit. In whatever endeavours they undertook, she would be a worthy opponent and staunch ally.

All he had to do was persuade her he did in fact love her as passionately as she desired.

❧

Amelia tried to curb her sobs. A grown woman of three and twenty, she was too old to be weeping like a baby. Taking deep breaths, she began to gain a modicum of control, which was immediately undermined by the tumult in her head.

Elbows on her knees, she rested her chin on her palms

and gazed out over the undulating landscape. It was midday, the autumnal light casting a golden aura over the earth. The sprawling trees were shedding the last of their leaves, carpeting the grass with cobweb-like jewels.

It was breathtakingly beautiful, and her heart cracked. Soon, she would never see it again. Her future, bleak as the encroaching winter.

Her sojourn here was over. It was time to return to Gresham Park, where her life would be spent managing the estate while fending off Ambrose's inept attentions. Unless of course he had found some other unsuspecting female in the interim; she could only hope.

Worse, she needed to tell Cate. Yet another person to whom the child had become close was saying goodbye. Her heart fractured a little more, tears brimming over and dripping down her cheeks. She tried to brush them away, but they kept falling.

A small hand crept into hers, and a curly head came to rest against her shoulder.

"Why are you crying, Mrs Dandelion?" Cate's question was delivered in a tremulous voice.

Amelia inhaled sharply, a shudder running through her. It took almost everything she had to speak calmly. To instil a bright note into her reply.

"'Tis nothing to fret about, sweetheart. Just some news, which caught me unawares. I will be fine, shortly."

Cate stretched up on tiptoes to plant a kiss on Amelia's wet cheek.

"There, there, all better now."

The child's trustingly innocent assumption, all ills could be assuaged with a simple kiss, shattered something deep within Amelia, and she was overcome by another bout of weeping.

"Mrs Dandelion, please do not cry."

Hearing panic in Cate's voice, Amelia drew in a desperate breath. "I-I'm s-sorry s-sweetheart, th-that did make it b-better. Th-thank you." She hugged the girl to her, scattering kisses over her face and making her chuckle.

"You are funny. I shall go and find Papa. He *always* knows what to do."

Before Amelia could stop her, Cate wriggled free and skipped over the lawns towards the house, yelling for her Papa.

She was met by Rupert coming in the opposite direction.

"Papa, Mrs Dandelion is sad."

"I know, Cate. I am going to talk to her."

An odd note in her father's voice prompted Cate to look at him suspiciously.

"Did you make her cry?" Hands on hips, her face creased in an angry frown.

"Not on purpose, but yes, I did."

If Amelia had taught him anything during the last few months, it was to be as honest as possible with Cate. The irony of that not lost on him.

"Make her smile, Papa, pleeeeeeease." Cate clung to his knees.

Rupert picked up his daughter and held her close. "I promise," he whispered in her ear. "Now pop off and find Lilly. Ask her to stay with you until dinner. Mrs Danneville and I need to have a chat."

Cate squeezed his cheeks in her chubby fingers and planted a kiss on his lips. "I love you, Papa."

"I love you more, precious. Run along."

Rupert stood her on the ground and ruffled her hair, waiting until she had run around to the kitchen entrance, before following in Amelia's footsteps.

He found Amelia staring out over the parkland. Her cheeks streaked with tears, her expression, desolate.

"Mrs Danneville, pray give me the chance to explain."

"You don't need to explain, Ru—my lord." Looking fixedly ahead, knowing she would break down again if she faced him.

"'Tis my own fault. To agree to your proposition without apprising you of who I really am was unfair. I will pack tonight and be out of your home tomorrow. I just need to tell Trotter." Her driver had settled comfortably into the household, and she knew he would also find it a wrench to leave.

Amelia's voice was empty, not even a hint of emotion.

Rupert could not bear it.

CHAPTER TEN

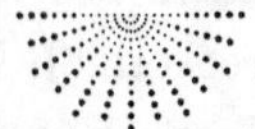

"My love, please look at me."

The endearment prompted Amelia to swivel around on the bench, her eyes widening in astonishment.

"W-what d-did you just s-say?" she stammered, certain her hearing was failing.

"My love," he repeated, daring to take her hand, and entwine their fingers.

"Amelia, I cannot tell you when I realised how deeply in love with you I am. It might have been when you laughed the evening we first met or when you told me Cate needed boundaries. It was possibly the day I watched you run barefoot over these lawns or when you argued with me about politics or society after dinner — every night."

He grinned as her expression became sheepish. "It might have been when you won my daughter's heart or when your hair unwinds at the end of a long day or simply when you smile at me. It might have been a single moment or all of them combined, but I do love you."

. . .

Amelia wondered whether she was dreaming. *He loved her? Was that even possible?* Her brow furrowed in bewilderment while she tried to make sense of it all.

"My first marriage was… let me just say, 'tis best forgotten. My wife was disinterested in our child and me. Her death, while sad for her family, regrettably had no impact on my life other than to release me from the fetters our union created. I was determined never to allow anyone close again.

"Then we met, and no matter how often I tried to erect a barrier between us, you kept crashing through it. Your efforts to appear plain and uninteresting failed dismally, and I had no idea why you would even need to. Your eyes sparkle like gemstones, and your skin is so soft."

He ran a finger along her jawline. "Your hair is glorious, even when you scrape it back into that God-awful bun, and all I want to do is tangle my fingers through it. My offer for marriage, although phrased without due consideration, is no less genuine. The only reason I did not admit how much I love you was because I had no mind to scare you away, and look how well I handled that…"

Rupert broke off, smiling tenderly, before doing what he wanted to do for many weeks. He slid his fingers into her hair, bringing her face close enough to brush her lips with his, even so slight a touch evoking a multitude of interesting sensations.

He pressed his forehead to hers. "Amelia Danneville or Ingram or whatever you are called, you have kindled a flame inside me, I thought long dead. One which burns so hot, I fear it may consume me. I do not care whether you are a scullery maid or a queen, I love you and want nothing more than to spend the rest of my life proving to you just how ardently."

. . .

Seconds ticked by, during which Amelia remained tongue-tied, but Rupert's words healed her battered heart. She drew back to search his face, seeing nothing but sincerity.

Finding her voice, she said, shyly, "Lord Lat—Rupert, I am truly sorry I kept my identity hidden. It was liberating for a while, to pretend I had no responsibilities and could travel the countryside without justifying my very existence.

"Unexpectedly, we met, and you seemed to like me for who I am not what my title could bring you. Then, there is Cate. Oh, how I love Cate. I had set aside my dream of motherhood. My marriage..." she faltered, then steadied herself, "...was never consummated. My relationship with Hayward was devoid of affection."

Her cheeks flushed bright red. "Hence my overly dramatic reaction to your proposal."

She paused, collecting her courage.

"Rupert, I do not know how long I have loved you, but when you declared I was suitable wife material, your words stung, and I recognised at some point you had stolen my heart. My impolite response aside, I maintain I do not wish to be considered *suitable* or *cared for*.

"I wish, nay demand, to be loved as though without me you would not be able to draw breath, and if this is the case, should you ever feel brave enough to repeat your proposal, I guarantee my answer will not be so long-winded."

She offered a tentative smile, her hazel eyes doubtful. *Was she expecting too much?*

Rupert held her gaze and brought his lips once more to hers, kissing her with an intoxicating sweetness — a long, leisurely kiss, which was neither suitable nor merely caring.

"Amelia, my love for you can never be extinguished. Now kindled, it may blaze fierce and hot or smoulder slow and simmering, but it will never burn out. My darling, will you marry me?"

Amelia stared at Rupert, drinking in his solemn features: the smoky grey of his eyes, the feel of his hand in hers, and the wonder of his kiss. There was never any real doubt.

"Yes."

One word, a heartfelt answer, yet Rupert's smile could have lit Badlesmere from the roof to the stables. He drew her close, resuming his seductive kiss before asking, "I presume you do not need anyone's permission?"

Their eyes met and both started to smile.

In unison they declared…

"Cate."

Three months later

Rupert stood in the library at Badlesmere, his gaze on his wife — of three weeks — and daughter in the garden, chuckling at their antics. He had just finished a long day with his stewards and was coming to see what his madcap family was up to. It was mid-winter. Snow blanketed the ground, yet there they were, wrapped in layers of clothes, making a snowman.

His mind wandered, and he reflected on the changes

meeting Amelia had wrought on his life. Changes he had not looked for but embraced with fervour.

Cate was ecstatic when asked whether she minded they marry, and begged permission to call Amelia, Mama, immediately. Occasionally, and to everyone's amusement, Cate still referred to her mother as Mrs Dandelion.

He and Cate had accompanied Amelia, first to her home and then onto Hungerford House. Amelia appeased her soon-to-be-former father-in-law by informing him she would transfer ownership of Gresham Park to him on the understanding he would not stand in the way of her marriage to Rupert.

Although short, the visit was, to Amelia's well-concealed amazement, pleasant. Lord Hungerford had declared he approved of Rupert, wholeheartedly, before mentioning, in an aside, he never liked Ambrose anyway.

Mr Archibald, pleased at the outcome of his visit, had persuaded Teresa's family that Cate was well cared for. With an added warning that should they pursue the matter further, he would have no alternative but to bring to light their daughter's transgressions. Disaster averted.

Laughter greeted Rupert when he pushed open the French door. The frigid air stung his face, making him gasp.

Cate spotted him and shrieked with glee.

"Papa. Papa." She ran to his side, seized his hand and tugged him over the frost-covered terrace to admire their genial, if somewhat lopsided, snowman.

"Please don't tell me that is my topper and scarf?" His

mock-horrified tones were met with gleeful giggles from his daughter.

"Fine, I won't." Amelia grinned up at her husband, who kissed her cold nose.

"Amelia, your face is like ice. Come on, you two, inside before you are as frozen as old Snowy here." Rupert hoisted Cate up onto his shoulders, then tucked Amelia's arm through his. The three strolled back into the house, chattering merrily, to be welcomed by a roaring fire and hot chocolate.

Amelia closed the door and drew the heavy curtains, shutting out the fading light. She turned to see Cate jigging about, thwarting all Rupert's attempts to divest her of her outer garments.

The scene caught her heart, and she breathed a contented sigh.

"Everything all right, my love?" Rupert who had finally wrangled Cate's boots off her feet, heard the soft sound. He glanced up and smiled gently.

The ever-smouldering spark kindled, and Amelia's countenance glowed with the depth of her love.

"Everything is absolutely perfect."

EXCERPT FROM UNRAVELLING ROANA

BROOKETON MANOR ~ AUGUST 1819

Gideon Dumont, 6th Earl of Brooketon, stared at the letter. The words made no sense. *Ro had left him?* He shook his head. Here was he rushing to their country estate, looking forward to spending what was left of the summer with his wife, only to find her missing, and no one seemed to know where she had gone.

How was this possible?

Where was she?

How could someone so vital, simply disappear?

He gripped the sheet and studied it for the fifth time.

Nothing had changed.

My darling, Gideon,

Darling! Am I entitled to call you that? You are to me. You always have been, and you always will be, so I shall grant myself one last indulgence.

If you are reading this, you know I am not at Brooketon

Manor. I do not expect you to forgive my flight, but I could not stay. The rumours, the whispers, the well-intentioned *comments have become untenable.*

I know many among our peers have affairs, kept under wraps, to scratch an itch their respective spouses seem unable to satisfy. I thought we were different. I thought we had a strong, loving marriage. I trusted, I hoped, I was enough.

Evidently, I was mistaken, and to think you found it necessary to seek another has broken me. I cannot stand by and watch the oaths we took disintegrate before my eyes.

For most of the last eight years we have been inseparable, yet I admit to being aware of a growing distance between us. Of late, you are never home and when you are, your mind is elsewhere. I can only presume, with her.

I miss sitting with you at the end of the day, engaging in lively conversation, or reading together. I miss taking constitutionals through one of the parks, or an exhilarating ride along Rotten Row. I miss your touch. Oh Gideon, I just miss you.

How tedious — a wife who wants to be with her husband.

Doubtless, I should be grateful for the brief happiness we shared — yes, eight years out of what I believed would be forever, is brief — but I am not. I am angry, hurt, disillusioned and betrayed.

If I was so lacking as a wife, why did you not talk to me? Legally, we are bound for life, but I am unable to live with your indifference.

In order to retain a shred of dignity, I have taken control of my destiny. Rather than air our problems in public, to the glee of the ton, I have let it be known I am wearied of city life and am retiring to the country for the foreseeable future.

Mayhap our separation will provide you the space and time to decide what or who you want. The fetters you obviously abhor no longer confining you.

Thank you for being the adoring husband you once were. I love you and will treasure the memory of what we shared.

Roana

The letter had an ominous finality to it. *Him... indifferent? Never! What was all this nonsense about affairs and fetters? Where the devil was she?* Admittedly, his arrival had been delayed by circumstances beyond his control, but this...?

With a muffled roar, Gideon flung the page on the desk, and stormed through the rambling old house to the domestic quarters. He burst through the baize door and down the corridor to the kitchens.

The staff, snatching a moment's peace to eat a meal, shot to their feet.

"M-my lord," Chambers, the butler, stammered. "How may I, we, be of service?"

The rest waited, nervously. All knew Lady Brooketon had departed. One was privy to the reason, and she was sworn to secrecy.

"Where is my wife?" Gideon barked the question, his face thunderous.

"I am afraid I have no idea." Chambers replied, his tone sincere. "She asked that only one small trunk and her valise be packed. She left about three weeks ago."

"Three weeks?" Gideon's mouth fell open in shock. "And none of you thought to apprise me of this?"

"We thought her ladyship had returned to London."

An understandable assumption given the earl's conspicuous absence from the Manor.

London could be stifling in the summer, and it was customary for members of the *ton* to escape to their country estates for the duration of the hot weather. Nestled in rural Dorsetshire, Brooketon Manor was a haven. At the beginning of August, every year for the past eight years, Gideon brought Roana here and, invariably, the couple stayed until the end of September.

In early July, when their mistress arrived on her own, the staff had been disquieted. Not entirely convinced by her assurances, his lordship would follow in a month as was their habit. For them to travel separately was unprecedented. Moreover, Lady Brooketon seemed unusually withdrawn and agitated.

A little over three weeks past, to their well-concealed astonishment, her ladyship had requested the carriage be prepared. Until the earl's unexpected arrival earlier that day, they presumed she was with him in the capital.

"Who drove her?"

"I took Lady Brooketon as far as Winchester. She bade me return, insisting she wanted to continue on to London by mail coach." Drake, the groom, piped up. Gideon's expression darkened — if that was possible — prompting Drake to add, "Forgive me, my lord. I did me darndest to persuade her, but her ladyship point blank refused."

Gideon was floored and, momentarily contemplated whether this was, in fact, a nightmare. One he hoped to God he would wake from imminently.

Where was she?

Even when not at the Manor, Roana was everywhere. In the carefully chosen furnishings, the whimsical touches, the light and colour. Before they wed it was a dreary place, somewhere Gideon rarely visited. Now they spent close to six months of every year here, spread around their responsibilities in the city.

He was on several parliamentary committees. Roana dedicated her days to all manner of causes. Her favourite was helping the archivists at the British Museum, cataloguing acquisitions. All were voluntary, but she was devoted to them.

A self-confessed bluestocking, Roana had never been comfortable or skilled at ladylike pastimes. She had mastered them, but the results ranged from passable to execrable. She preferred books, history, and the outdoors, to sewing, dancing, and singing, although she enjoyed listening to music.

These were the things Gideon loved about her and he *did* love her. Her accusation he was involved in a dalliance with another woman cut him to the quick. He had been faithful to Roana from the moment he clapped eyes on her. She beguiled him, with her flaming auburn hair, sparkling green eyes, and vibrant personality.

While he retraced his steps through the house in search of any hint as to Roana's whereabouts, he recalled how she ticked him off for teasing, and alleged he was in his cups the first time he told her she was beautiful. He had been unaware her family considered her unprepossessing and the least marriageable of her siblings.

He had met Roana when she ran into him, literally, while trying to avoid some elderly viscount who thought she would submit to his advances. Gideon implied he was her escort for the evening, effectively discouraging the ardent gentleman.

Roana thanked him and they fell to chatting. Gideon was entranced by Roana's intelligence and her wit. That, to him, she was the most ravishing woman he had ever seen, merely a bonus.

His family tried to dissuade Gideon's suit, hoping he might find a more suitable bride. Roana's... idiosyncrasies were well-known. The handsome young man who had recently turned four and twenty was considered very eligible. Roana, at barely ten and eight, would find another swain.

Gideon was not to be thwarted, and dedicated every spare moment to courting Roana who, it was obvious, returned his affection. Before long, he had persuaded Roana, his love for her was the forever kind. He was the second son of duke, an earl in his own right. She, the youngest daughter of an earl. Their match was, reluctantly, approved.

They were married three months later.

That was nearly nine years ago and, as Roana's letter stated, the couple had been inseparable ever since.

Now, believing he had betrayed her love, she had vanished into thin air.

ABOUT THE AUTHOR

Rosie Chapel lives in Perth, Australia with her hubby and three furkids. When not writing, she loves catching up with friends, burying herself in a book (or three), discovering the wonders of Western Australia, or — and the best — a quiet evening at home with her husband, enjoying a glass of wine and a movie.

Website: www.rosiechapel.com

A Christmas Prayer *with Ashlee Shades*

The Lady's Wager

Winning Emma

A Love Impossible

Unravelling Roana

Fairy Tale Romance

Chasing Bluebells

Contemporary Romances

Of Ruins and Romance

All At Once It's You

Cobweb Dreams

Just One Step

His Heart's Second Sigh

The Pomegranate Tree

Hannah's Heirloom - Book One

Hoping to trace the origins of an ancient ruby clasp, a gift from her long dead grandmother, Hannah Wilson travels to the fortress of Masada with her best friend, Max. Strange dreams concerning a rebel ambush begin to haunt Hannah and following a tragic accident, she slips into the world of Ancient Masada.

A woman out of time, Hannah must rely on her instincts and her knowledge of what will befall this citadel to survive. Will she escape, or is she doomed to die along with hundreds of others as Masada falls – and what does any of this have to do with an ancient ruby clasp?

Echoes of Stone and Fire

Hannah's Heirloom - Book Two

Pompeii - a vibrant city lost in time following the AD79 eruption of Vesuvius. Now rediscovered, archaeologists yearn for an opportunity to uncover the town's past. Some things, however, are best left alone - revealing the secrets hidden beneath the stones could prove perilous. Hannah and Max are brought to Pompeii by a surprise invitation to join an excavation team who are trying to uncover the city's long history.

After entering an excavated house that bears a Hebrew inscription, Hannah's two worlds collide, and she falls back through time to ancient Pompeii. A place where her ancestor is a physician to gladiators engaged in mortal combat, where riotous mobs run amok and where a ghost from the past returns to haunt her.

Will Hannah and her loved ones manage to escape the devastation she knows is coming, before the town is engulfed in volcanic ash? Will she ever find her way back to Max the love of her life, waiting not so patiently millennia away? Or will echoes be all that remain?

Embers of Destiny

Hannah's Heirloom - Book Three

AD80 - Hannah and Maxentius must embark on a new journey to Northern Britannia. This harsh frontier is far from the comforts of Rome and danger lurks where least expected; a garrison of soldiers, some unhappy with their isolated posting; local tribes, outwardly accepting of their Roman occupier, but who may still resent the seizure of their lands.

Millennia away, Hannah Vallier finds a familiar item while working in a museum near Hadrian's Wall. It is the pomegranate; carved by Maxentius on Masada. Before Hannah can discuss it with Max, disaster strikes! Believing her husband has been killed, Hannah retreats into the past, her soul melding with that of her ancestor, but with little idea of what they could face. Is the risk from the conquered tribes, or much closer to home?

As rebellion threatens to shatter a fragile peace, Hannah's heart whispers that just maybe Max isn't dead and that he is calling her home. Can she trust her heart, or will she remain caught out of time, her destiny floating away like embers on a breeze?

Etched in Starlight

Hannah's Heirloom - Prequel

Maxentius - a Roman soldier fresh from the battlefields of Armenia, arrives to take command of the military outpost of Masada, Herod's isolated citadel in the Judaean desert. A seemingly mundane posting after years of warfare, Maxentius finds it more challenging to maintain a focused garrison than to face the wrath of the Parthians across a disputed frontier.

Hannah - a young Hebrew physician spends her days dealing with injuries from street brawls, deprivation, disease and loss. As her beloved Jerusalem plunges into chaos, her brother — who belongs to a band of rebels determined to drive out their Roman occupiers — tells her of their plans to storm a desert fortress and steal the weapons stored there, persuading his reluctant sister to go with him.

Masada - following the ambush, Hannah finds and treats three badly wounded Roman soldiers. In the aftermath and against impossible odds, Hannah and Maxentius realise that they are more than healer and captive, their fate already etched in starlight.

Prelude to Fate

For Lucia, staring into the jaws of an horrific death, escape seems impossible.

Rufius Atellus, a veteran Roman soldier, is appalled when he recognises one of the victims about to be executed. Surely this is a ghastly mistake?

A ferocious she-wolf, anticipating a tasty meal, suddenly finds herself under a human's control.

In an unexpected twist, and as danger threatens, the lives of all three become inextricably entwined.

Was it chance brought them together in that theatre of bloodshed, or simply a prelude to fate?

Legacy of Flame and Ash

An unremarkable family ring — lost when its owner was killed in the catastrophic eruption of Vesuvius — is excavated after nearly two millennia buried under tons of lava, setting off an extraordinary sequence of events.

A brazen robbery, and the ring is lost again. The theft and subsequent investigation, inspire twelve-year-old Cristiano Rossi to dedicate his life to the search and recovery of stolen artefacts.

Fast forward twenty years. Whispers of a rare item being offered for sale on the black market, initiates a joint operation between the Italian and British branches of the, colloquially named, Art Squad.

Hannah Vallier and her tech savvy assistant, Bryony Emerson — whose abilities to track down the untraceable, led to them assisting the UK Art and Antiquities Unit — have unearthed an intriguing thread. Reluctantly, Cristiano agrees to team up with the pair to thwart the traffickers, retrieve the artefact and, hopefully, dismantle the site.

What ought to be a routine assignment is complicated by a rogue operative, an unexpected romance, an ancient connection, and a *very* angry ghost!

Once Upon An Earl

Linen and Lace - Book One

When Fate saw fit to intervene in the life of Giles Trevallier, the very respectable Earl of Winchester, by dropping a female — soaked to the skin and with no memory of who she is or how she came to be there — literally at his feet, no one could have predicted the outcome.

While uncovering her identity, Giles realises he is falling hopelessly in love with his mystery guest, who unbeknownst to him, is succumbing to similar emotions; but, when the heart is involved, a thoughtless word or gesture can thwart even Fate's best-laid plans.

Faced with misunderstandings, whispers of scandal, secret documents and foreign agents, their chance at a happy ever after seems elusive, but fairy tales often happen when least expected, and love — however inconvenient — usually finds a way to conquer all.

To Unlock Her Heart

Linen and Lace - Book Two

Abused by a duke, and shunned by Society, relief seems at hand when Grace Aldeburgh is bequeathed a house in a small village, far from malicious gossips.

Once there, a tentative friendship blooms between Grace and Theo Elliott, the local doctor, who has already resolved to be the man to unlock her heart.

Just when happiness appears to be within her grasp, her erstwhile tormentor once again stalks Grace. After a failed kidnap attempt, the duke's quest culminates in an acrimonious confrontation, and the reason for his venal pursuit becomes agonisingly clear.

NB: This book contains adult themes and situations which, although minimal might be a trigger for some.

Love on a Winter's Tide

Linen and Lace - Book Three

Every day, Helena disappears into a world few acknowledge, helping the poor, downtrodden, and abused. A husband is the last thing she can be bothered with.

Busy managing his shipping line, Hugh Drummond sees no need for a wife, whose only joy is dancing and frivolity. If — and it was a huge if — he ever married, it would be to a woman as capable as he, not some giddy society Miss.

Then, Hugh meets Helena and despite their resolve, fate, it seems, has other ideas. As their attraction deepens however, treachery threatens to tear them apart. Will they uncover the perpetrator in time, or will their love be swept away, lost forever on a winter's tide?

A Love Unquenchable

Linen and Lace - Book Four

Jessica Drummond, a bright and cheerful young woman, rarely gives romance, let alone love, a thought. Long hours working in her brother's shipping office affords little chance of her ever meeting an eligible bachelor.

Duncan Barrington, veteran of the Napoleonic Wars, believes himself wounded in both body and soul. He has no intention of inflicting his demons on anyone, certainly not a beautiful and, in his opinion, irresponsible city lady.

One cold and snowy morning, the plight of a bedraggled puppy throws Jessica and Duncan together and, as a spark of something indefinable yet wholly unquenchable begins to burn, it is unclear who rescued whom.

A Hidden Rose

Refusing to suffer the humiliation of her husband flaunting his mistress at Society events, the newly married Duchess of Wallingstead, Ella Lennox, takes control of her life. She leaves London for the family's country seat in remote Yorkshire.

A woman alone, Ella spends the next four years turning a cold, grim house into a home, and transforming the fortunes of the estate. Not afraid of hard work, she soon earns the respect of those around her with her determination and unconventional attitude.

Out of the blue, the duke arrives. Resigned to another arduous visit, Ella is stunned when it seems he is attempting to court her.

Impossible!

Could her dream of a happy marriage be about to come true?

Everything hangs on a snowstorm, a herd of cows and an uninvited guest.

Rescuing Her Knight

The *de Wiltons* – Book One

A story, invented to keep a little girl distracted, marks the beginning of another tale. One destined to remain unfinished for twenty years.

At thirteen, Adam Marchmain became Kitty de Wilton's 'Knight of the Garden' — a title bestowed following an accident which resulted in six-year-old Kitty having her knee sutured. Kitty never forgot his gallantry, but pledges made as children rarely survive into adulthood.

Their paths separated until Fate decreed, they meet again.

Widowed, badly disfigured and his sight ruined, Adam returns to his family home, a shadow of his former self.

Similarly afflicted, although her scars are invisible, Kitty — against her better judgement — is persuaded to help Adam banish his demons. This requires a subterfuge which, if discovered, might shatter more than the bonds of friendship forged two decades previously.

To Kitty, determined to break through the shield Adam has erected, the risk is worth it.

To see his smile and hear his laughter.

To rescue the knight of her childhood.

Just when a fairy tale ending is within her grasp, Kitty is threatened by the man who murdered her husband. In a cruel twist the tables are turned, and Kitty is the one who needs rescuing.

His Fiery Hoyden

A Novella

Livvy has no respect for the nobility; they let her down when she most needed them. Why should she accede to their demands now?

Philip, Lord Harrington, is stunned to discover the young heir to the dukedom lives a stone's throw away in a ramshackle cottage, and resolves to restore the child to his birthright.

They meet in a clash of wills, but just when it seems Livvy might surrender, the victory Philip desires, may not taste all that sweet.

A Regency Duet

Luck be a Pirate

Luck wasn't something retired pirate Kennet Alexson believed in – good or bad. However, even he had to concede that landing a job at Trentams shipyard, and meeting Lynette Collins, was more than coincidence.

Fortune it seemed, was smiling on him for once.

As Kennet adjusts to life on dry land, his friendship with Lynette deepens into something far more enduring, and what once seemed elusive now becomes possible.

Unfortunately, fate has other plans, and Kennet's good luck is about to run out.

The Highwayman's Kiss

Surrendered Hearts – Book One

Nothing exciting had ever happened to Juliette St Clair. Her days were spent assisting her father or calling on friends, wandering art galleries, taking constitutionals or, and more preferably, escaping into her books. Her evenings her evenings — an endless round of balls, where she preferred to remain invisible.

Until the day she was robbed by a highwayman.

A Regency Christmas Double

Heart Rescued

Four years since Jasper lost the woman he was hoping to marry. Four years since he closed his heart and withdrew from Society. He has no idea his reclusive existence is about to be shattered.

Enter his sister's best friend, Harriet, a flame haired beauty, who needs his help.

Reluctantly he agrees and as they spend time together, it is clear their feelings run deep. Although Harriet affects Jasper in a way no woman ever has, he believes her to be out of his league ~ but it's Christmas and she might just be the one to melt his frozen heart

Catch a Snowflake

Romance often blossoms in the most unlikely of places - but in a ward full of wounded soldiers - surely not?

When Lucas Withers comes face to face with Jemima Parsons - a young woman who blames him for her brother's injury - falling in love is the last thing on their minds. What neither of them anticipated, was the magic of snowflakes.

Fate is Curious

A Novella

Happily, ever after? No such thing! Bereft, following her beloved husband's sudden death, Lady Charlotte Sherbrooke has lost her belief in such romantic nonsense.

Successful shipping merchant, Zacharie Romain, is no stranger to loss; his business can be hazardous. Moreover, his wife died in childbirth and even though it happened a decade ago, he has no mind to expose himself to such sorrow again.

They meet in less than joyful circumstances but, as the year turns and grief diminishes, the woes of a small boy become the catalyst for something wholly unexpected. Can Charlotte and Zacharie trust what Fate has in store or will past heartbreak prevent them from taking a chance on love?

A Christmas Prayer

with Ashlee Shades

A Short Story

An entreaty from a frightened child.

Orphaned and only nine, Caroline Thorne has to grow up before her time. She is doing everything she can to keep what is left of her family together and out of the workhouse but is terrified her prayers are not being heard. Or maybe they are…

A petition from a woman desperate for a family.

A chance meeting with three orphaned siblings, tugs at Elizabeth Barrington's heart strings. Thus far, she and her husband have not been blessed with children and, as Christmas approaches, a plan begins to form - one which might just be the answer to her prayers.

Two Christmas prayers, as different as they are the same.

Will they hear and, more importantly, heed the answer?

The Lady's Wager

Surrendered Hearts- Book Two

A Novelette

Ged Mowbray will do anything to avoid being married off to the suitable prospects his parents insist on parading in front of him.

Melissa Bouchard is under no illusion her sizeable dowry is the attraction to suitors, not her.

An overheard conversation leads to an offer too good to refuse, but what happens when a lady's wager, becomes a gamble on the happily ever after, you did not even realise you wanted?

Winning Emma

Surrendered Hearts - Book Three

A Novelette

Randolph Craythorpe — earl, covert operative, and occasional highwayman — believed his dalliance with Lady Felicity Hartwich would lead to marriage. It did, but not to him! The arrival of an unwelcome guest, however, provides the perfect opportunity to indulge in a little retaliation.

Emma Newbury accompanies her cousin, Lady Charity Anscombe, to London for the Christmas season. Once there, she comes face to face with the three men who witnessed the humiliating aftermath of her father's disgrace — one of whom, to her irritation, has taken up residence in her dreams.

Their infrequent encounters only serve to confuse but, while winter tightens its grip on the city, what was inconceivable becomes the one thing for which they both yearn, yet bound by Society's rules, cannot admit.

As the snow falls, Randolph begins to understand that to win Emma, he will have to surrender.

A Love Impossible

A Regency M/M Novelette

Tasked with investigating a heinous crime, Edward Lindsay travels from London to Dublin — a city which holds too many memories — in the guise of guardian to his sister. He knew it could be hazardous, and relished the challenge, but that wasn't what caused his stomach to tighten as they approached landfall.

Dublin held more than just a murderer.

There was also Aidan.

While attending a party, Aidan Griffen is astonished when he comes face to face with a man who fled Dublin two years previously. A man he has desperately tried to forget.

As Edward closes in on his quarry, a fire, deliberately extinguished, is rekindled. But what of it? Edward and Aidan share a love impossible, and to acknowledge their feelings — more dangerous than confronting a killer.

Is there any hope of a happily ever after?

Unravelling Roana

A Regency Novelette

Tired of being ignored by her husband, Roana Dumont, Countess of Brooketon does the one thing guaranteed to get his attention. She runs away… to Venice, leaving behind a set of riddles for him to solve… *if* he feels their marriage is worth saving.

Gideon Dumont, 6th Earl of Brooketon is flabbergasted when he discovers his wife has apparently vanished off the face of the earth. A series of puzzles, the only clue as to her whereabouts.

The question is… will he unravel them?

Chasing Bluebells

A Fairy Tale Novella

Once upon a time, somewhere in France, there was a man whose reckless obsession led him down a dark path — one which, ultimately, cost him his life. That ought to have been the end of it. Regrettably, as is so often the case, those who least deserve it, suffer for the actions of others.

A decade after being sent away, Sebastien Daviau returns to the little village where everything began. Hoping to lay the ghosts of his childhood to rest, he studiously ignores the possibility, he might run into Charlotte de Montbeliard.

As luck would have it, Charlotte is the one who runs into him… well, his horse… and although the brief encounter leaves a lasting impression, neither recognises the other.

A name revealed causes a freak accident, catapulting Sebastien's past into his present, and bringing him face to face with a man whose reputation would intimidate the most ardent of suitors.

Can whatever is blossoming between Charlotte and Sebastien survive the challenge imposed, or is their happily ever after about to fade as quickly as the bluebells they loved to chase?

Of Ruins and Romance

Kassandra Winters has intrigued Gabriel St Germain since he accidentally knocked her flying outside her university professor's office. Her face haunts his dreams, yet he never expected to see her again. So, he is surprised when she appears, as though destined to do so, in the middle of a ruin, and he concocts a plan to win her heart.

Gabriel's old-fashioned courtship touches something deep inside Kassie and, although struggling to believe someone as handsome as Gabriel could possibly be interested in her, she soon realises she has fallen irrevocably in love with him. However, just as Kassie shares everything of herself with Gabriel, her world comes crashing down.

Can their romance survive, or will it fall in ruins, like the relics of antiquity that brought them together?

All At Once It's You

When Alex arrives in the small village of Rosedale Abbey, to take up a position as a research assistant for a renowned archaeologist, the last thing she is looking for, or expects to find, is love.

Jake was perfectly happy with the status quo. When it came to relationships, he didn't do committed or long term. He called the shots, and if his current flame didn't like it, she knew what to do. A philosophy, which served him well - until he met Alex.

Romance blooms, but even as the untamed wilderness of the North Yorkshire moors weaves its spell, a long-buried secret might yet jeopardise their happily ever after.

Cobweb Dreams

A Novella

A holiday on the Scottish isle of Mull was just the break Chloe Shepherd needed, an escape from her boring office job and her complete lack of anything resembling a social life. Romance, it seems, isn't on the cards and, although Chloe dreams of finding her soulmate she is beginning to believe love is like cobwebs — spun overnight, only to vanish in the early morning breeze.

Under sufferance, Dominic Winters makes a flying visit to Mull to check on a rental property owned by his family. He hasn't got time for this — so indulging in a holiday fling is the last thing on his mind.

A lamb stuck in a bog proves a most unexpected matchmaker and, while Mull weaves its magic, Chloe wonders whether those fragile cobwebs might be far more stubborn than she thought.

Just One Step

A Short Story

In the aftermath of an horrific car accident, Daisy Forrester travels to Italy - hoping, so far from her memories, she might begin to heal.

Archaeologist, and single father, Adam Willoughby is too busy looking after his young daughter to give romance let alone love, a thought.

Neither expects a chance encounter in an ancient ruin to be anything more, but sometimes, that's all it takes.

His Heart's Second Sigh

A Novella

Reuben Faulkner and Paige Latimer are two happily single people, who have no desire to upset the status quo.

Unexpectedly, they are thrown together, only to discover both want far more than a casual friendship.

Just when things take an interesting turn, Reuben's past catches up with them, and threatens to derail their blossoming romance before it has chance to start.